CASH & CARY

MEN OF MEMPHIS BLUES SERIES, BOOK 1

SAM E. KRAEMER

This book is an original work of fiction. Names, characters, places, incidents, and events are either the product of the author's imagination or used fictitiously. Any resemblance to actual persons, living or dead, business establishments, events, or locales is entirely coincidental.

Copyright © 2021 by Sam E. Kraemer
Cover design: Arden O'Keefe, KSL Designs
Editing: Sandra D., One Love Editing
Formatting: Leslie Copeland, LesCourt Author Services
Proofreading: Beau LeFebvre, Alphabitz Editing
Published by Kaye-Klub Publishing, 2021

These characters are the author's original creations, and the events herein are the author's sole property. All rights reserved. No part of this book may be reproduced, scanned, or distributed in any form, printed or electronic, without the express permission of the author. Please do not participate in or encourage piracy of copyrighted materials in violation of the author's rights. Purchase only authorized editions.

All products/brand names mentioned in this work of fiction are registered trademarks owned by their respective holders/corporations/owners. No trademark infringement intended.

THEIR STORY

Cash Mitchell—

Cary Brewer is the best catcher in the country, and he's part of the reason I'm starting my first Major League Baseball game for the Memphis Blues. He told me the first day of our minicamp that he'd make my life a living hell. Oh, he achieved that goal in spades, but I doubt in the way he intended.

Tragedy never takes a holiday, and having suffered one, I'm not ready for another. When it happens, Cary is there to support me. I have a guardian angel who's been looking out for me, and I never knew it.

Now, I wonder what the cost will be for both of us—since I've already fallen for him.

Cary Brewer—

Skip Mitchell told me that his nephew is a hell of a pitcher. Seeing the kid in action proves the man right. But when I lay eyes on Cash Mitchell, my gut ties itself in knots. Ask anyone—I'm not *that* guy.

The attraction I'm fighting tooth and claw will only be detrimental to both of our careers. I need to get away from him, but how do I do that?

The kid has me completely under his spell, and the blue in my uniform will match the blue in my pants if something doesn't give.

This work of fiction is approximately 55,000 words in length, ends in an HEA, and can be read as a standalone novel.

PROLOGUE
CASH MITCHELL

I was bent over the toilet in one of the bathroom stalls in the locker room, damn sure I was going to die since I'd already been puking for at least five minutes. It was the pitching coach's visit that had set me off.

I'd just started to suit up for my first start in Major League Baseball as the newest member of the Memphis Blues. It had been my life's goal to make it to the big leagues, and there I was, puking in the bathroom like a fucking wuss.

The clacking sound of cleats on the navy floor tile of the bathroom had me heaving again, but I had nothing left to give. "Kid! You got about ten minutes to get yourself out there. I don't know if you know it or not, but it's time to go to work! The game can't start if there's nobody to pitch the fucking ball to the batter."

The deep bass of the man's voice echoed off the subway tile of the bathroom's walls, and had I not been trying to stop dry heaving, I'd have laughed at the commanding sound. It was Cary Brewer, the more than seasoned catcher for the Blues, and he was as gruff and outspoken as anyone I'd ever met. He'd made it known during training camp that he was going to make my life a living hell, and so far he'd been true to his word.

I wiped my mouth with the towel I'd grabbed when I'd entered the locker room to puke, and I lifted my foot to flush the toilet. I didn't have my cleats on yet; I'd been dressing when the pitching coach sat down next to me on the bench by my assigned locker.

"*I wouldn't get too fuckin' comfortable here, Mitchell. I didn't want ya on the team in the first place, and when you get out there and choke like you always do, we'll ship your ass back to Nashville.*

"*I'll get the pitcher I want, and you'll be a bad memory. I'm sure nobody will notice you can't pitch a changeup worth a damn, and that's what you're gonna need against Garcia.*

"*Don't forget that he bats third, so you oughta be resting comfortably back in the bullpen in record time. Enjoy your hour as a starting pitcher for the Memphis Blues,*" Roger Hardy had stated in a husky voice only I could hear. My stomach immediately flipped, and I took off like a fucking gunshot to the toilet, not thinking I'd ever be able to stop heaving.

I wiped my mouth again before I walked out of the stall and over to the sink, grateful I didn't have my jersey on yet. I rinsed my mouth a few times before I wiped across my face with the back of my hand since the towel was gross. I tossed it in the laundry cart in the corner on my way out.

When I turned around to leave, Cary Brewer stepped in front of me and held out a sports drink and two antacids. "Take these and then small sips of this. What did Hardy say?"

I was too fucking scared to respond. They were all a team and had been for a long time. I was the new kid nobody knew shit about except that I was called up from the Triple-A farm team in Nashville at the behest of the head coach, Dutch Weingarten. He'd gone over Roger Hardy's head and straight to the general manager, Sandy James, to suggest me. That sin wouldn't easily be forgiven.

My uncle, Skip Mitchell, had been a scout for the Miami Sharks where Weingarten had been the pitching coach before I ever picked up a glove. Uncle Skip had followed my career from the first time I'd picked up a baseball, and he'd been my biggest cheerleader, especially after my father died from being hit by a car while working for the highway department in Florida where I'd grown up.

Uncle Skip attended my games when he was in town, and when I got to high school, he started taping my games when I was pitching. I knew for a fact that the coaching staff of the Blues knew I'd come to the attention of the head coach because of my uncle, and they all fucking resented it. The players weren't friendly, either, but Uncle Skip had told me I could win them over if I just showed them I could carry my weight and do my job. I wasn't so sure he was right.

I popped the chalk tablets and took the drink. "Thanks. What's it matter? Hell, you told me you'd make my life a living hell, so I doubt you'll be too sorry when I'm sent back down to Nashville." Without waiting for a response, I headed out of the bathroom to get ready for the game.

I sat down on the bench again to finish getting ready for my debut in my first regular-season game. I'd done well in preseason, but Hardy was right. The changeup was my fucking kryptonite.

Sandy James came into the locker room with the coaching staff and gave a quick pep talk, and then we were all out of the locker room and onto the field to warm up. After drills, I headed to the bullpen to warm up my arm.

I was surprised to see Cary Brewer at the other end of the pen talking to one of the bullpen catchers. The two of them were laughing as Brewer put on his pads and bumped fists. I looked out to the field and saw the other bullpen catcher in the box warming up the team instead of Brewer.

"This ain't vacation time, kid," I heard Brewer yell at me—not for the first time—so I reached for the rosin bag and clapped it a few times before I went to the wire basket and grabbed a ball, scuffing the ball in my hands as I considered what the fuck I was really doing there. I could hear the crowd assembling, and I knew the St. Louis Steamboats had already warmed up before us. I could hear the slap of the ball in the catcher's mitt across the field as the pitchers warmed up, and I felt my stomach roll again.

I saw Brewer hold up his fist and jog toward me, so I walked midway to meet him. "What's wrong, kid?"

"I can't do it." I felt the tears well up in my eyes, but I fought them hard. It was then I really missed my dad. I'd only been eight when he was killed, but I remembered playing little league and hearing his voice from the sidelines cheering for me, even when I didn't do well. I'd missed that voice every time I picked up a glove.

Brewer chuckled. "You're not gonna let us down on this, are ya? Skip has been singing your praises long enough he oughta get a goddamn Grammy. You gonna make him look like a fool? Hell, I watched your films and went to bat for you, as well. You got somethin', kid. Don't make us look like we don't know our asses from a hole in a bathroom wall," Brewer snapped before he spit on the ground.

I looked down to see sunflower shells, and I started laughing. "Not tobacco?" I challenged.

"Fuck no! I got nice teeth that cost me a small fuckin' fortune. Now, shall we play, or do you want the name of my goddamn dentist?" Just like that, the tension was broken.

"Alright, I'm ready. Let's warm up," I agreed, watching his sexy ass in his royal blue pants as he jogged back down the line before he took his squat. He signaled the pitches, and I threw them, straight down the line and right into his mitt—even the goddamn breaking ball that was new to me. We had chemistry, Cary Brewer and me. It felt good to see the nod of his head at the sound of leather on leather. It made me proud to see him grin with approval as he threw the pill back to me. It felt like I was playing catch with an old friend.

Something in my mind told me I wanted to know more about the man. I had a feeling the more I knew, the more I'd want, and that would be problematic. Cary Brewer wasn't gay, and I wasn't out, anyway.

CHAPTER ONE

CARY BREWER

I ran up the back steps from the beach and stopped to rinse my feet. Running on the beach every morning was me-time, and I needed it. The house I was leasing in Fort Myers for the winter was like a damn dream. It was on the Gulf side of Florida, and hurricane season had been kind, thankfully.

I'd been there since the end of the regular season, licking my wounds for the way things ended. The season had started out mediocre, but as Cash Mitchell had gotten more comfortable on the mound, things had taken a positive turn, and everyone kept whispering "World Series." Fucking jinxes.

We thought we'd earned a wild card berth in postseason, but the fates turned against us at the end, and it simply wasn't meant to be. Cash had a great season, but the rest of the team wasn't in the groove, and I was sure there would be changes made in the off-season. I was ready to retire, but Dutch had asked me to give them one more year to help the kid get his sea legs, and Sandy James had thrown in a nice preretirement kicker, so I agreed to stay on.

I had been making a list of shit I wanted to do when I

finally left the game—first off was to get fucking laid on American soil. It had been a long time since that had happened.

Nope. I wasn't out, but then again, not many current professional athletes in the US were these days. Many former sports figures had come out after they'd retired, and I was planning to be among that number, but I had to hold off for one more season—my last.

When the need for sexual satisfaction became too strong to be satisfied by my friend Lefty, I flew to an island somewhere that I wasn't easily recognized, and I procured the services of a professional. It was a means to an end, and I could wait until after my career ended to chase some American tail. Hell, I was so used to being alone, I'd probably never have a real relationship of any kind, but at least after I retired, I could get laid without it making headlines.

I could hear my phone blaring on the white quartz counter inside the little ocean-blue beach house, so I quickly rushed inside, trying not to fall and break my damn neck on the tile since my feet were still wet. I grabbed my cell and answered without looking at the screen to see who was calling. "Yeah?"

"Cary?"

Only one person called me Cary. "Cash?" There was a horrible sound before the kid coughed. "Cash, what's wrong?"

The kid and I had actually become friends over the season. He was a hell of a pitcher, but he doubted his abilities, and fucking Roger Hardy fed his insecurities at every opportunity. I'd told Dutch if he wanted Cash to do well, he needed to shut Hardy the fuck up or fire his ass, but the front office rarely listened to the players, the pricks.

I heard another sniff. "Kid, what's going on? Where are you?" I pressed.

"I'm home… in Tampa. My uncle Skip died yesterday. My mom's too upset to make arrangements, and I'm not sure what to do," Cash explained. I heard him trying to control his emotions, and I felt so awful for him. Sadly, I'd had to deal with that shit when my little brother and parents died. I was an old hat at making funeral arrangements.

"Hell, kid! Give me the address where you are, and I'll be there as quick as I can. Just calm down a little and take care of your mom. I'm on my way." A few minutes and sentences later, and we hung up.

For reasons I couldn't understand, I was drawn to Cash by an uncontrollable force. The kid had gotten under my skin and had started to haunt my dreams, and there seemed to be no end in sight to what I'd do for him. I didn't know what the fuck was wrong with me.

Hell, in the spirit of getting myself some distance from him, I'd been pushing the other guys to lighten up and get to know him better. I'd hosted everybody at my house for cookouts and shit during the season so they could all get acquainted away from the pressures of the job. It seemed to have worked.

Plans were in the works to get the group together for a snowmobiling trip before spring training started in February, and I was actually looking forward to going. I still wasn't sure if it was the best idea to let the guy who had never seen snow plan the trip, but Tito Arroyo, our new first baseman from Cuba by way of Miami, had jumped at the chance to organize it, and I hated making travel arrangements.

As I took a shower, I thought about the purpose of the trip I was about to take to Tampa. My history with Skip Mitchell went back to the beginning of my career. Skip had been on staff as a scout for the Miami Sharks back then, and he'd been instrumental in getting me called up after part of a season on the farm team all those years ago. I owed the man my career, because without him, I'd have had a difficult time catching the eye of the front office as a catcher with a .240 batting average.

Most likely, I'd have quit the sport rather than play ball in the summer and work a seasonal construction job as most of the guys in Triple-A ball had to do.

I got along well with Skip, and when he'd called me to talk about Cash and then sent me the film on the kid when he was in high school, I knew Cash was a shoo-in for the National Pitcher of the Year his senior year at Florida State. When Cash was picked up out of college by Memphis' farm team, the Nashville Blue Notes, Skip kept me in the loop about what was happening with the boy.

I watched Cash's skills strengthen over his first year with the Blue Notes, and I became more impressed as the season progressed. That winter, after Skip and I determined the kid was ready, I went directly to Dutch with his stats and everything Skip had sent me on the kid because I knew the Blues had been looking for a pitcher like Cash Mitchell for several years. We just had to wait for Cash Mitchell to grow up.

I was then reminded of our age difference—Cash was twenty-two, and I was a lot older than twenty-two. The thoughts I'd been having about the guy during his rookie season weren't what I'd expected. I found myself spending time with Cash under any ruse I could manufacture. One night toward the end of the season, Skip had called me. That was a conversation I'd never forget, especially now that my friend was dead.

"The team looked good yesterday, Brewer. You and my nephew are a hell of a duo! It was damn near a no-hitter. You two are in sync like no other pitcher and catcher in the league right now. He looks up to you, man, and I trust you won't ever let him down, even if one of you leaves the Blues.

"I tried to be around for Cash as much as possible, but you know how scouting is. I was on the road a lot, and after Stew got hit by that car, Carole just kinda left the kid to raise himself because she was grieving hard. I hope I've been a good role *model for him, but he still needs someone to guide him. I'm glad he's got somebody solid like you to have his back, Brewer."*

That conversation would haunt me the rest of my life as I measured it against the news of his death. Could he have already known something was wrong with him and was trying to tell me?

As I packed my shit to head out to Tampa, I realized Cash hadn't mentioned what had taken Skip's life. I had the feeling it wasn't anything sudden. I think Skip knew he wasn't going to be around for Cash, and now that he was gone, it was left to me to be the kid's support system. *No fuckin' pressure...*

I pulled in front of the yellow clapboard house with the white trim on Hillsborough Bay. As I took in the sight of the area, it was exactly the way Cash had described it so many times when we were on the road. There were pumpkins on the porch, and multicolor mums and fall flowering baskets were decorating the porch railings. It looked like a typical home in a nice neighborhood, unlike the shithole where I'd grown up in Detroit. My childhood with two fucking addicts wasn't what I wanted to dwell on at the moment.

I hopped out of my SUV and straightened my white button-up shirt, khakis, and navy sports jacket as I walked up to the porch, checking my short blond hair in the storm door. I was glad I'd gone to get my hair cut the previous week because I didn't even think twice about taking off when the kid had called. At least I looked respectable, even if the thoughts I had about Cash Mitchell were completely indecent.

I pressed the doorbell and waited for someone to open the door, feeling the nerves settle in my gut. I'd never met the mother, and I'd started feeling more nervous as I'd driven the hour and a half from Fort Myers to Tampa Bay.

The front door opened, and a thin woman dressed in a black sweater and skirt offered a sad smile. "How can I help you?" she asked. I could see the resemblance to Cash, so I guessed it was Carole Mitchell, Cash's mother.

"Hello. I'm Cary Brewer. I play for the Blues with Cash. Is he around?" I asked, feeling more self-conscious than I had in a very long time.

"Oh, Mr. Brewer, come in, please. Cash is out for a run, but he'll be back soon. Would you like something to drink? I have coffee, tea, wine, beer," the woman offered. Considering it was only eleven in the morning, it seemed a bit early for wine or beer, but the glazed-over look in her eyes told me she'd been imbibing for a while. When she stumbled as she walked toward what I was guessing was the kitchen, I became worried about what I'd walked into.

"Uh, coffee is fine, Mrs. Mitchell. Please don't go to any trouble." I glanced around the kitchen, and I could see everything was in perfect order. Maybe it was an accident that she stumbled?

She poured me a mug of coffee and put it on the table with a watery smile. "I'm sorry we're meeting under these circumstances. Skip has talked about you for years, and when I talk to Cash, he tells me how kind you've been to him. He said you helped him find his new apartment?"

When Cash arrived in Memphis at the beginning of the season, Skip set him up in corporate-style, ugly-as-shit furnished apartment, and it cost a fucking arm and a leg. When I found out where the kid was living, I started asking other players who I knew had recently bought single-family homes after contracts were renewed and they knew they'd be staying in Memphis for a few years.

Thankfully, Andy Chaves and his wife, Tracy, had lived in a nice town house near the stadium before they bought their new big-ass house outside of town. They talked to the management company where they used to live and got the kid a great deal. I helped him move the few things he had with him, and Danita, one of the event planners in the front office, gave Cash some furniture she had inherited when her mother died. The pieces had definitely belonged to an older lady—pink-and-blue-flowered sofa, pink velvet chair, and fancy oak table and chairs—but the kid gladly took it and made a donation to Danita's favorite charity after she refused to let him pay for it.

Cash wasn't fussy about shit, which was refreshing from a young guy. When we brought the furniture into his new place, he didn't bitch about it for a minute. As I had glanced around the living room when I'd entered Mrs. Mitchell's home, I noticed the furniture looked damn close to the stuff in Cash's town house. I was guessing he didn't worry about it because the furniture reminded him of his childhood home.

Mrs. Mitchell put a basket of muffins on the table between us as she sat down across from me. I could see that what was in her coffee mug wasn't coffee, but I kept my mouth shut. It definitely wasn't my business how anyone dealt with their grief. Until someone went through it themselves, they couldn't begin to predict how they'd react to losing someone they loved and depended upon for support.

When my parents and little brother died in a house fire in Detroit while I was in college at Ann Arbor, Michigan, I didn't process my grief for a long time. After my family was buried and the fire was ruled to be an accident due to my father cooking meth in the kitchen as I'd suspected, I went back to school, business as usual.

It took several years—and a really shitty season—before I finally sought help to handle the huge loss that had consumed me for years. I had to reconcile it within myself that I couldn't have changed anything if I'd been there. My parents had made their decisions, and nobody could have changed their minds. I'd called DCFS on my parents more than once to get Kenny away from them, but social services had given him back every time, only barely carrying out an investigation into what I'd told them.

"I didn't get a chance to ask Cash, but how did Skip die?" I asked as I sipped my coffee.

Mrs. Mitchell reached into the sleeve of her plain black sweater and retrieved a ladies' handkerchief, dabbing under her eyes to keep the tears from falling. I could see she'd been crying, and I wondered if it was smart for Cash to have left her alone while he went for a run.

"He was diagnosed with pancreatic cancer back in early spring. He wouldn't let me tell Cash or anyone, really. He had his will prepared, and I guess he got to die his way with nobody around to cry for him as far as I know.

"Skip was a very private person, and he didn't share personal stories with me, nor with Cash, I don't think. He came to visit us here, but he never stayed at the house, and he never mentioned any ladies in his life, so I don't know much about what his life was like in Miami.

"We got a call this morning from an attorney who is representing Skip's estate, and Cash has to meet with the man sometime today to find out Skip's last wishes regarding his burial. Perhaps you could go with him? I just can't do it all again," Mrs. Mitchell stated.

I nodded. I could completely relate to that feeling. Losing people that you love had a way of hardening a person's heart, which was probably why I hadn't bothered to date anyone since I'd gone to college. I'd had a fuck buddy back then, but he got tired of living in the closet because I played baseball and couldn't be out. After my family died, I'd refused to allow him to go to Detroit with me, and that was the last straw for him. We broke up and never spoke again.

I graduated from college with a degree in finance and the next day did a walk-on tryout for the Detroit Steel. They picked me up and promptly traded me to Miami, which was where I met Skip. Without him, who knew where I'd have ended up?

There were pounding footsteps coming from the back deck that faced the bay. The door opened, and I saw the look on Cash's face when he spotted me sitting at his mother's kitchen table—pure relief. I stood and walked over to him, pulling the kid into a hug because I could see he needed it more than anyone I'd ever met in my life. His brown hair was sweaty, which matched with what his mother had said about him going for a run.

"Are you okay?" I whispered as he held tightly to me. I could feel his body convulsing, which reminded me of his puking session before his first game back in April. Common sense said to let him go so he didn't puke on me, but his grip on me was so tight, I couldn't have pried him off. I heard him suck in a breath, and then I knew he was sobbing.

"I know, Cash. Skip loved you so much, and he was so proud of you," I whispered, patting his back and hoping like hell I was offering any comfort at all. I couldn't say how long we stood there, but he finally pulled away and opened a drawer under the kitchen countertop, retrieving some tissues. He wiped his eyes and blew his nose as he stared at me.

I felt like he wanted some sort of an explanation for Skip's death, but of course, I had no answers. I glanced around the blue kitchen to see his mother had left the room, so I pulled her vacated chair out and helped Cash sit down.

"You want some water?" I asked.

Cash shook his head. "I just finished some before I came inside. I'm sorry to call you like I did."

"*No!* Don't you dare worry about that. Skip was a friend of mine, and I'd have found out about it eventually. I'm so sorry he died. I didn't realize he was sick. He'd never said anything about it in all the times we've talked," I explained, wanting to reach for his hand but deciding it might be inappropriate, so I placed my hands on my lap and relaxed a little, taking in the dark circles under Cash's eyes and blotches on his tanned skin. I could tell he hadn't been sleeping, and I wondered how long he'd been in Tampa and why he hadn't called me sooner. Last I knew, he was going on vacation with a couple of friends from college. I'd been missing him so much, and he'd been right down the road? *Son of a...*

CHAPTER TWO

CASH MITCHELL

I knew I owed Cary an explanation about why I was at my mother's instead of in Cabo as I'd led him to believe. I'd told him I was going on vacation with friends from college because I didn't want to sound pathetic that I had nothing to do in the off-season. He'd said he was going to hide out for a couple of months and none of us should call him unless it was a fucking emergency. We'd all laughed, but I was sure he was serious, which was why I was kicking my own ass for calling Cash when we'd got the call from a neighbor in Miami to say Uncle Skip had died.

I hadn't even known he was ill. Mom had known about it for months, but she'd lied to me, saying Skip had gone on a recruiting trip to Asia, which was why I hadn't heard from him. Stupid fool that I was, I believed her.

I'd learned that Uncle Skip had been under hospice care for three months. He'd been diagnosed in May, and he'd sworn Mom to secrecy about his condition and how long he had to live. I guess he thought I was too fragile to handle the news, and that pissed me off.

His lawyer had flown up to Tampa from Miami and was coming over to the house to talk to me, mentioning I was Skip's sole heir for his possessions when we made the arrangements to meet. I'd rather have had Skip back than anything he could have left for me.

The man had already done so much for me as a kid growing up without a dad. He'd come to Tampa when he had time, and then when I started playing ball, he'd made as many games as he could. Uncle Skip always supported anything I'd wanted to do, never failing to tell me I could be or do anything I set my mind to accomplish. He always told me I was exactly like my dad, his older brother, and how proud my father would be of me. There were times when I was growing up that those words were all that kept me going.

Thanks to Uncle Skip, I had a great agent who had negotiated a fantastic contract for me, so I didn't need money. His advice to me was worth all the money in the world. Uncle Skip had also told me to trust Cary's intuition and listen to him when I started with the Blues, and I had. That was before Skip found out he was dying, so the fact he'd made a point of showing me how much he respected Cary meant more to me now than Uncle Skip could have ever known.

The Blues had had a hot and cold year, but I was proud that my rookie stats set a new club record: a 3.62 ERA (earned run average), and a 1.14 WHIP (walks plus hits per inning pitched), with 143 strikeouts in 121.2 innings. Skip had sent me a cookie bouquet when he found out I'd had a one-hitter win over the Boston Pilots, and I'd gladly shared it with the team.

When I sent Skip an email that we didn't get into the playoffs, he told me that I couldn't change the past, so I should concentrate on the future. Another bit of good advice. I wasn't sure what I was going to do without his endless encouragement. I would definitely feel the loss of him in my life.

I got out of the shower and quickly checked my phone to see I had a missed call from the lawyer, so I wrapped a towel around my waist and called the man back. "This is Cash Mitchell calling for Mr. Lawson," I responded when the phone was answered.

"Thank you for calling me back, Mr. Mitchell. It's me, Oren Lawson. I was wondering what time I could come by and if you'd give me your address again? I lost the paper I'd written it on," the man offered. I gave him Mom's address and got dressed. I wasn't sure what the man had to tell me.

Knock! Knock! "Cash, man, everything okay?" I was then reminded that Cary was there to be with me, and suddenly, I felt as if I could handle anything.

Cary parked the rental car outside the players' parking lot behind Wrigley Field. "You sure they'll let us in?" I asked. It was Uncle Skip's wish to be sprinkled in the bullpen of Wrigley Field. He'd been a die-hard Chicago fan—he and my father had grown up in Chicago, and Skip had been a bat-boy for the team as a kid. He'd asked for the nearly impossible, and I was afraid I wouldn't be able to give it to him.

Of course, Cary was able to call in enough favors until we got to one of the groundskeepers at the ballpark who had known Uncle Skip and was willing to allow us to fulfill that last request. The man was meeting us at the field under the cloak of darkness to allow us to lay Uncle Skip to rest in his favorite place on earth. I would be forever in Cary's debt for all of his efforts.

We waited by the fence surrounding the parking lot of the

ball field until a golf cart pulled up to the gate and flashed its lights twice before the gate opened automatically. I saw a hulking man step out of the cart, and I felt my blood run cold. "Who is *this* guy?"

"He's one of the groundskeepers. It's a ten-minute task, and I've got five C-notes in my pocket. Just be cool, kid," Cary whispered.

The large African American man walked over and stared at us for a moment before Cary spoke up. "Hi. I'm Cary Brewer, and this is Cash Mitchell. I spoke to Ray Hawkins at the suggestion of..."

"...of Austin Jarvis. I'm Ray Hawkins, head groundskeeper. If you'll get into the cart, we'll get started." The man pointed to the cart, so I turned to look at Cary. He winked, grabbed my hand, and we were off.

Austin Jarvis was the third-base coach who'd played college ball with Rashad Odami, a left fielder for the Baltimore Pirates. After that, the trail got a bit too convoluted for me to follow, but I'd estimated it took about eight different people to get me ten minutes in the Breeze's bullpen of Wrigley Field. I didn't know what I'd have done without Cary to make it happen. I would be eternally grateful to each person involved.

Mr. Hawkins drove the cart through the tunnel and around the field to the bullpen. The lights were on in the stadium, which I hadn't expected, and I saw a group of people standing inside the enclosure where I'd expected to see no one. I turned to Cary, who smiled. "Everyone in the league knew Skip. A few people wanted to pay their respects since they found out he's died. I didn't think you'd object." I had to fight hard to keep from kissing him.

We got out of the cart, me carrying the bronze urn where Uncle Skip's ashes had been placed after the cremation that had upset my mother. Apparently, Skip and my dad, Stew, had been raised Catholic, and the religion wasn't fond of the scattering of ashes. Mom had said it was just like Skip to buck tradition. I'd laughed. We'd never attended any church of any religion, so I had no idea why it fucking mattered.

Mr. Hawkins followed behind us as Cary opened the gate to the bullpen, and I was surprised to see how many people had actually gathered there. We followed Mr. Hawkins over to where someone was waiting in a suit who looked very official.

"Gentlemen, this is Reverend Eustice Clark. He's the chaplain for the team, and Mr. Martino asked if he'd mind saying a prayer," Mr. Hawkins explained. Lou Martino was the general manager for the Breeze, and as I looked around, I saw the man standing with Sandy James, the GM for the Blues. There were a few players I recognized, past and present, but it was mostly front-office types there to see off Uncle Skip. I knew he'd be laughing his ass off if he were watching from somewhere, seeing all of the suits had come out to remember him.

After the prayer by Reverend Clark, I'd been allowed to sprinkle Skip's ashes around the perimeter of the bullpen, and then waiters came in with trays of shot glasses containing brown liquor—good Kentucky bourbon if I were guessing right. It was Uncle Skip's drink of choice. Thankfully, Cary stepped forward to offer the toast instead of waiting for me to try to figure out what to say.

"Here's to Skip Mitchell. He lived his life for this game. He's brought all of you some of the best players baseball has ever seen. May the heavens be so lucky to have Skip recruiting for them. To Skip..."

"To Skip..."

My eyes were filled with tears at how beautiful it all really was, so I drank down the liquor in honor of a man I would miss as much as my own father. It was like I'd been blessed with two dads, and I'd be forever grateful.

Cary and I were invited up to the owner's box for an impromptu cocktail party in Skip's honor, and when he dragged me out of the building at three o'clock on Sunday morning, I felt we'd given Uncle Skip a proper send-off. Cary hadn't had anything to drink after the first toast, so he was able to drive us back and pour my drunk ass into my room in the suite he'd booked us at a fancy hotel downtown.

"I'll leave the bathroom light on in case you have the urge to puke," Cary teased as I sat on the side of the bed to take off my shoes.

"I ate. I don't think I'll puke." I damn well didn't want to think about it too much to keep from provoking my stomach into proving me wrong.

"Good," he responded as he went into the bathroom and returned with a trash can.

I giggled. "Did you know about that? That they were gonna do that? The S-S-Sharks didn't do s-s-shit for him." Yeah, it was all slurred. Cary bent forward and began unbuttoning my shirt, helping me off with it before he pulled me to stand, placing my hands on his shoulders.

We were nose to nose, which was the first time I'd noticed we were the same height. If I wanted to kiss him, I just needed to pucker up. Just as I started to lean forward with my lips in a sexy pucker, Cary looked down as he unbuckled my belt, and my kiss met the top of his head.

"Easy, kiddo. Let's get you comfortable so you can pass out. I'm going to change our flight back to Tampa tomorrow. You might wanna sleep in. Let me get you some aspirin and water, and then I'll leave you alone." Cary was being too kind to me.

Oh, I didn't want him to leave me alone, and when his thumb grazed my thickening cock through my boxer briefs as he slid my pants down, I wanted to grab his hand and hold it there where I could rub against him for friction. I wanted the feel of someone's hands on me other than my own, and feeling Cary touch me would be a dream come true.

He placed his palm against my solar plexus and gently pushed, causing me to fall backward on the bed. "You wanna get in with me?" *Where the hell did that come from?*

Cary laughed. "No way! I don't want to be an unknowing target if all that bourbon makes a reappearance." He was making a joke, but...

"Take me on a date. I haven't been on a date in forever," I whispered before it all went black.

I opened my eyes and sat upright in bed, looking around the room I didn't recognize. My head was at a dull ache, but the taste in my mouth reminded me that I'd had whiskey the previous night. I didn't drink hard liquor often—never during the season—but when I was with Uncle Skip, well... Then I remembered what I'd done the previous night and who had come with me. Hell, who had been the one to make it possible.

I slowly got out of bed and went into the bathroom to start my day. After a quick shower, I pulled on jeans and a Blues T-shirt and went out into the common room to see a pot of coffee on the large dining table in the middle of the room. The television wasn't on, and as I listened, the large suite was dead silent.

"*Cary?*" No answer.

I walked to the other bedroom to see his suitcase was on the bed, half-packed, but he was nowhere to be seen. I picked up the shirt he'd worn the previous night to Wrigley Field and smelled it. The scent was like spice and clean sweat, which was exactly what I found extremely attractive about Cary.

Everything about the man was sexy. Some girl somewhere had to be so fucking lucky to get to date him. If I ever found a guy like him, I'd tell everyone to fuck themselves and hang on to the man like a lifeboat on the *Titanic*.

I wanted to climb into Cary's unmade bed and roll around in the sheets so I could cover myself with his scent like a dog in the yard. If I ever got his smell all over me, I'd never shower again.

I heard the lock on the door of the suite make a grinding sound before it opened, so I hurried into the sitting room and hopped onto the couch, putting my feet up and grabbing a tourism magazine from the side table. I pretended to be deep into an article about a ghost and gangster tour of Chicago. "Wow, next time we're here, I wanna do this." I turned the magazine for him to see what I was reading... pretending to read. No way in hell did I even want to leave the hotel room if I was ever in Chicago again with Cary.

I finally looked up to see the gorgeous man was shirtless, and his hair was wet. I felt the air rush out of my chest, and I fought my instincts to reach out and pull him onto my lap. I wanted to lick him clean and get him sweaty again.

"Where'd you go?" It came out before I could stop it, and it was pretty stupid because clearly, he'd gone to work out.

"Took a run. I figured you'd still be asleep." Cary wiped his chest with his T-shirt, and I nearly swallowed my tongue.

"I didn't drink *that* much last night. Besides, I had aspirins and water. Anyway, what time is our flight? I wanna get Mom a souvenir. She's never been to Chicago," I lied. Mom had started traveling with a group of friends when I'd started college, especially during baseball season. She refused to go to my games because she claimed she couldn't bear for me to be distracted to the point of getting injured by trying to impress her, and I learned to live with the fact she'd hated baseball her whole life. Neither of us ever brought it up.

Cary chuckled, his deep voice surrounding me like a warm blanket. "Are you going to get her something with a *date* on it?"

I turned to him, hoping he wasn't having a stroke. "What do you..."

"Take me on a date. I haven't been on a date in forever."

Oh no...

CHAPTER THREE

CARY

The look on the kid's face was priceless. Goddamn, he was so cute, and I just couldn't resist teasing him. I knew he'd been overserved at the little get-together the Breeze had hosted in honor of Skip, but the stubborn guy wasn't about to admit it. Teasing him about it was fun, but I didn't really want to embarrass him too much.

"I'm just kidding you, kid. Why didn't you go to Cabo with your friends from college?" I went to my suitcase and grabbed some clean clothes for the trip home. I seriously doubted the Breeze would have been so agreeable about letting Cash sprinkle Skip's ashes in the bullpen had they not won the World Series the weekend before Skip passed. I could definitely tell they were still riding the high of the win.

Lou Martino had even cornered me about when I thought I might retire and whether I would consider coming on board the Breeze organization as an assistant coach. I'd explained to him that I needed to give the Blues one more year, but after, I'd sit down and have a discussion with the front office. I had no idea what I'd do after my baseball career was over, but maybe coaching was in my future? At least I'd have an option I'd never considered.

I went into the bathroom and pushed the door almost all the way closed so I could shower. "*So, Cabo?*" I yelled as I adjusted the water and finished stripping. I stepped into the stall and began washing, loving the water pressure on my shoulders. I'd tossed and turned all night, having a hard time getting to sleep because Cash was in the other room in the suite, and I wanted to be with him so damn much. It didn't have to be sex, but just holding him would have been perfect. In the process of castigating myself for my carnal thoughts the previous night, I'd wrenched my neck.

"Honestly? I didn't really make friends in high school or college. In high school, I was the weird skinny kid who could pitch a baseball pretty damn fast, but in college, I just didn't really fit in with any of the different cliques on campus—even the jocks," Cash explained from the doorway.

He continued. "I was pretty shy back then, and I didn't really try to make friends because I just wanted to concentrate on baseball and academics. Some of the guys on the team were jealous that I got to play so much, so they did shit like flush my jock down the toilet or steal my clothes when I was in the showers. They gave me shit about the fact coach knew my Uncle Skip, and they said he gave me preferential treatment, but he really didn't. I worked hard for my spot and my grades, but nobody wanted anything to do with me, really. I definitely haven't talked to anyone from the team since our last game after graduation."

I quickly soaped up my body before stepping under the spray to rinse off. I glanced into the mirror across from the shower to see Cash studying me. Our eyes met, and his face flushed before he walked away. Did his face turn red because

I'd caught him watching me or because he liked what he'd seen?

Thinking back on the season, I'd noticed Cash never looked around in the showers after games, but then again, I didn't either, really. Occupational hazard of being a gay man in a sport filled with jocks.

I loved my teammates, but I'd never consider fucking one of them—well, one, but knowing Skip now depended on me to be the surrogate uncle in his absence, it was fucking creepy to think about the kid that way. He just had a crush on me. Without encouragement, he'd get over it.

An hour later, we were in the rental on the way to the airport. "So how come a good-looking guy like you doesn't have an off-season girlfriend?" I asked before I could stop myself.

I quickly recovered. "I know a lot of guys, especially the young ones, like to concentrate during the season, but usually they like to cuddle up to a pretty girl in the off-season. They have a girlfriend from October to February.

"You should get out and burn off some steam, kid. Baseball is a pressure cooker, as you saw at the end of the season." It was the best advice I could offer as the surrogate uncle.

"I've got plenty of time for dating. Sorry I said that last night. I had too much to drink. It won't happen again." Cash's voice trailed off, but I didn't want him to feel bad.

I glanced to the side to see he looked upset. "Kid, yes, right now, you've got baseball on the brain, but you need to have some fun. You gotta find a way to relax or you'll get a damn ulcer."

I pulled into the rental car garage, and we hopped out. I grabbed my bag, and Cash grabbed his, and we went to check in for our flight. Thankfully, we cleared security easily with nobody recognizing either of us—not that I thought they would. We were in Breeze country, and I doubted anyone gave a shit about two players from the Memphis Blues, especially with both of us wearing Blues baseball caps and sunglasses.

Once we were settled in first class, Cash turned to me. "What do you do for fun? Do you have an off-season girlfriend?"

I chuckled. "I usually go travel for a month and find a few friends with benefits to tide me over. I don't fuck around during the season," I confessed, with ninety-percent honesty.

"Ah. Where... Do you have friends somewhere else?" Cash pressed, the nosy little bastard.

"I have all the friends my money can buy." My comment was rather offhanded before I pulled my cap down and kicked back my seat to take a nap. Not sleeping the night before was catching up with me. I was tired as fuck.

We got off the plane and headed toward the main terminal and the parking garage. "Let me drop you off before I drive back to Fort Myers," I offered.

Cash was silent for a moment before he cleared his throat. "I think I'll just take a cab to keep from holding you up. Guess I'll see you when we're both back in Memphis before we head to spring training. I gotta go to Miami to handle Uncle Skip's estate, so I won't be able to go on the trip to wherever everyone was going. I'm not really a snow person, anyway."

"You want me to go with you? I'm fine without going as well." *Please, say yes!*

"Thanks, but I need to do this by myself. Have a nice holiday." Cash took off down the dirty yellow hallway toward the taxi stand. I wanted to argue with him and force him to allow me to come along to Miami, but I could see by the look on his face that anything I said would just make him more upset and embarrassed.

I probably shouldn't have teased him about his date comment when he was less than sober. He seemed like a sensitive guy, and I was now his support system. I'd give him a week, and then I'd go see him and maybe take him out for dinner. We could get over the awkwardness and get back to being mentor/worshipful protégé. It wouldn't be a date, no matter how much I wanted it to be.

Maybe I'd slip off to Cozumel or Tijuana for a long weekend after we got shit straightened out? Getting a little release and a fresh attitude sounded like a plan.

October winds were warm in Fort Myers, and I wanted to feel the cool breeze when I went for a run, so I hauled my nuts back to Memphis sooner than I'd planned, not motivated enough to bring myself to plan a trip to Mexico or anywhere else to fuck a stranger. I kept the house in Fort Myers in case I wanted to go back at Christmas, but it felt good to be home.

I did a few projects around the house to keep me busy, weeding out crap I'd shoved in the garage that I'd held on to for years. Most of it was the secondhand furniture I'd accumulated while I was in college, and I'd taken it with me when I was in Triple-A ball because I had dick else to my fucking name. It was actually bittersweet to have it hauled away.

Back then, I'd worked part-time at a consignment shop, helping load and unload things people dropped off, and I'd been given first choice of what was available. I was grateful people were willing to donate the things they no longer needed for someone else to use because at the time, *I* was the *someone else* who needed help.

I paid it forward, donating all of the furniture to a women's shelter in Memphis. As I watched the shit being hauled out, I felt my eyes well up at the memories that were going along with all of it.

Those pieces of furniture had held my gratitude for someone's generosity at donating the items to give me somewhere to sit or put down a cup when I was in my rookie year in the farm league. They'd held me when I worried that I'd never see my dream of being a Major League Baseball player come true. I'd been borne under the weight of my parents' addictions and most likely would have headed down that road myself if I didn't have the ability to read batters and call the pitches to win the games. That furniture had *physically* held me when I cried on the anniversary of my little brother's birthday and relived the suffocating guilt at not being able to save him. I'd failed Kenny all his life, and that wasn't something I would ever forget or get over.

Once the movers left, I sat in my house, staring into space. For the first time in a long time, I felt lonely, so after I'd run out of things to do, I'd tempted the guys with barbecue from a place we all loved if they'd come over on Sunday to watch football.

I'd called Cash to invite him over, assuming he was back from Miami, but he didn't answer. After two more weeks and no word from Cash, I decided to call Carole, his mother, to check on her.

"Hello?" I'd called the landline at her home in Tampa, but the voice that answered wasn't Carole or Cash.

"Hi, is Mrs. Mitchell around? It's Cary Brewer, a friend of her son." I never felt comfortable introducing myself to anyone over the phone.

"Oh, hi! This is Kim Donlyn. You're one of Cash's baseball friends, aren't you? The two of them aren't here right now—I mean, Cash and Carole. They went to run errands, but I can take a message and have one of them call you back." The stranger's voice was actually quite friendly.

"Is Cash okay? I've been trying to get in touch with him for a few weeks, and his number goes directly to voicemail every time. I, uh, I'm worried about him." My heart was actually beating out of my chest, which wasn't usual.

I was worried, and I couldn't help myself. Why was Cash avoiding me? Was his cold shoulder because I'd stupidly teased him about the date comment? And who the fuck was the guy on the phone?

"Oh, he lost his phone in the ocean. We... I live in South Beach, and Cash wanted to go deep-sea fishing, so I got a friend of mine to take a group of us out. Cash ended up falling off the boat while he was trying to pull in a *huge* tarpon. Damn thing weighed more than a hundred pounds, and Cash wasn't prepared for how much of a fight it gave him. He's waiting to get a new phone until he heads back to Memphis," the stranger, Kim Donlyn, explained. It didn't make me feel any better that he hadn't found another way to check in with me.

"Is he okay? Did he get Skip's things handled?" It was really none of my fucking business, but I couldn't stop myself from asking. I felt jealous, and I didn't really understand why.

The guy chuckled. "Cash decided to hang on to the Miami condo. I, uh, I live nearby, and I've introduced him to some of my friends. He's been having a great time down there.

"We came up to Tampa to drop off some things for Carole that Skipper wanted her to have, and then we're going back to Miami for Christmas. Oh! You should join us. I bet Cash would love it if you came for a visit during the holidays." Who the fuck was this Kim guy? Was he...? Were they...?

I, however, was shocked at the man's outright bluster at inviting me to come to Miami for a visit without getting Cash's permission. I didn't know the jackoff on the phone, and I didn't know what he was to Cash, but my gut was telling me I *needed* to know. I needed answers, by god, and I was fighting with myself not to cancel my Sunday party and get on a plane to Tampa—or maybe Miami.

"Are you and Cash close?" Yes, I was prying, but I couldn't help myself.

There was a high-pitched giggle. "Oh, honey, not nearly as close as a lot of other people would like to be, but he's a sweet, sweet boy. I can have him call you when he gets back. He took Carole to the salon, and then he was going to the home improvement store to get some supplies to repair the roof. A storm came through, and some shingles were torn off. Cash and I are going to get up there and fix it tomorrow."

I just couldn't help myself. "When did you meet…"

"Oh, the gang's here, so I need to go. I'll tell Cash to give you a call, sugar. So long." With that, the guy hung up the phone.

I sure as fuck didn't like the idea of some guy spending time with Cash when I wanted to. The kid was sweet and kind and naïve. He wasn't worldly by any stretch of the imagination. He was twenty-four, and having met his mother and knowing Skip, the kid had lived a somewhat sheltered life. I'd be damned if I'd let someone take advantage of him if I could do anything to protect him.

Later that Saturday evening, I called Andy Chaves, the star shortstop for the Blues, who had the sweetest wife in the world. "Yo, Brew! What's up, my friend?"

"Hey, man, I need to cancel Football Sunday," I explained, having already made an airline reservation to fly to Tampa.

"Everything okay?" Andy asked. He and his wife, Tracy, were expecting their first baby at Christmas. Tracy was a chef, and she'd worked as an apprentice at some fancy restaurants in New York when she met Andy. She wanted to open her own place someday, but she'd told me she was waiting until they had a more stable future, which I could completely understand.

The past two Sundays, Tracy had brought over a ton of food in addition to the dozens of wings or pounds of barbecue I'd ordered in for Football Sunday, even though I told her not to bother.

As I was about to cancel the gathering, I remembered I'd still have to pay for the food I'd ordered because I'd missed the cancellation window of more than twenty-four hours. If I could send it somewhere else, maybe all wouldn't be lost?

Unfortunately, my head was all over the place, and I had no idea how the fuck to get a grip on myself. Most of all, I wasn't sure why I felt the need to hotfoot it down to Florida to check on Cash. Yes, I was attracted to him, but it was ridiculous to feel so fucking possessive. I had no hold over him, and that wasn't who I was supposed to be in his life.

"Not really. I need to go out of town to check on a friend," I stated.

A hand definitely went over the speaker on Andy's end of the line, and then a Peanuts-like, muffled, conversation took place before it was suddenly very quiet. "You still there?" Andy asked.

Andy Chaves was an incredible, intelligent guy. He'd grown up in the Philippines until he was twelve, but he had dual citizenship because his mother was an American. His family had traveled extensively because his father was some sort of scientist, and Andy had actually attended college in England.

He'd played ball in Japan for several years until he was scouted by the New York Liberty and brought to the US to play shortstop for them, but that all occurred before the Blues' GM, Sandy James, decided to trade a much-sought-after, pain-in-the-ass third baseman to the Liberty to bring Andy to Memphis.

I'd called it the second-best deal Sandy had ever made. The first was calling up Cash Mitchell. Andy, Tracy, and I had hung out together in the off-season, and while I didn't really talk about my personal life, I had the feeling Andy knew I was gay.

"Yeah. I realize it's short notice, but if you and Tracy wanna host it here, the food can still be delivered, and Tracy doesn't have to bring anything. I'll get..."

"Dude, hold up. Where are you going?" Andy asked.

I sighed. I'd really avoided having close friends because the life of a baseball player was fucking transient for most of us, unless someone was a franchise maker—Jeter, A-Rod, Ripken. Come to think of it, I'd been with the Blues long enough that I supposed I could be considered a franchise player, though not a franchise maker.

Maybe it was time to open up a little? The way I saw it, I had one year left with the Blues, and now I had a quasi-offer on the table from the Breeze for a coaching job. Was I ready to come out?

"I'm going to Tampa or Miami. Cash is dealing with Skip's estate, and I don't like him doing it alone. I'll leave the key under..."

Andy cut me off. "Cary, man, I talked to the kid a few weeks ago. He and I got to be friends during the season because we worked out in the early mornings together, and we'd take batting practice together so he could get his average up. You know fucking Hardy was on his ass all the goddamn time." No, I hadn't known that for sure because Cash never said a word. I wanted to confront Cash about why he had remained silent on this piece of information, but my gut told me the kid was trying to show he could handle his shit, and I couldn't make him believe I doubted him.

Andy then continued. "I called to check on him after I heard about Skip. He told me about sprinkling Skip's ashes at Wrigley. Dude, seriously? I'd have flown to Chicago for the thing you guys did if you'd told me.

"You know, a lot of us are good guys, and we don't give a damn who anyone rolls over to in the morning. You believe me, right?" Andy confirmed what I'd always believed about most of the guys on the team.

Of course, I knew they were great guys, but I had no idea about Cash taking extra batting practice. "When in the hell... Why didn't Cash tell me he needed batting practice?"

Andy chuckled. "Dude, seriously? He didn't want any of the guys to know, but he really didn't want *you* to know. He's... Hell, Brew, it's not for me to say, but he didn't want to do anything that would make you think less of him. The kid worries about what people think of him—you more than others—and he wanted to impress you with his batting skills. Mitchell idolizes you, dumbass."

I was floored. My whole reason for remaining in the closet was based solely on my fear of people rejecting me because I was gay. I'd had parents who I'd told about being gay when I was in middle school and look how that shit turned out.

I'd always wondered if they became addicted to drugs because they couldn't accept they had a gay son. After I told them, Mom ended up pregnant with Kenny not three months later. They didn't really talk to me much after that, and from then forward, I'd felt invisible in my home.

It was always there at the front of my mind—the self-doubt and fear that people would hate me if they knew I liked cock. Add in the guilt I felt over my brother's death at the hands of my parents and their addiction because I was a disappointment, and I felt like the lowest of the low. Maybe it was time to go back to the shrink?

"I'm sorry I didn't include anyone, Andy. I mean, I didn't think about it at the time, and that's my bad, but I just wanted Cash to be able to do what Skip wanted him to do. Look, I think you know about me, and thanks for never asking me about it. I just... I just never wanted to chance that people would turn their backs on me," I confessed without specifics.

Andy cleared his throat. "Brew, man, everybody feels like they're being judged for one reason or another. We all have our own shit we're afraid people will hold against us, but true friends will love you regardless—if you let them. You're so damn guarded, and I kinda believe I know why, but I won't put a label on you. If you want to tell me something, then I wanna listen. I give you my word that I won't tell anyone." He was completely sincere, and it was nice to hear.

Of course, I knew better than to say anything over the phone. The fucking tabloids would give a left nut to get info like that on a professional athlete, and as much as I trusted Andy, I wasn't willing to take the chance. "I'll wait to leave till Monday. Come over tomorrow and tell your wife not to make food this time. I've got it covered, okay?"

"Okay, Brew. See you at noon," Andy agreed.

We hung up, and I sat back on the couch, second-guessing my decision. If word got out about my orientation and reached the front office, it would be bad. If word got out and reached the media, my life was over. I wasn't ready to be the poster boy for gay athletes.

I looked around my living room to see the saddle-tan leather furniture I'd bought. Every seat was a recliner, and it was a single man's dream come true. The walls were a soft cream color, and there was a beautiful rug that took up most of the room. It was some sort of faded design that was still very colorful, and I really liked it. All of it was new. None of it held any memories for me because the lady at the furniture place who came to my place to figure out the interior décor had picked it all.

There was nothing personal to see—no pictures of my dead family. No family heirlooms. No special memories from my childhood or my college life to remind me of happy times. It was pretty fucking sad as I thought about it. It was also the typical behavior of someone who kept everyone at arm's length.

When my teammates—more acquaintances than friends—came over to my place for Football Sunday, they saw nothing that gave them any insight into the real me. They saw what I wanted them to see—a bachelor with no ties to anyone, just as I'd been most of my life.

It all made me wonder what the fuck did I really want out of life? Did I want to meet someone and make it permanent, and if I did, how could I make them fit into what I was willing to share about my life? I wasn't prepared to be a permanent fixture anywhere, I decided as I gazed around my place. How the hell could I, as a professional baseball player, go looking for love?

Instead of going to bed as I probably should have done, I went to my home gym and ran on the treadmill for at least an hour as I attempted to sort out my head. It didn't really help. Skip had trusted me to take up where he'd left off with Cash, offering support and advice as it became necessary.

I couldn't be the pitcher's mentor and romantically pursue him at the same time. Oh, I wanted him badly, but I wanted his best interests to be the most important things, and I just couldn't reconcile the two schools of thought.

How to meet both needs wasn't clear, but I was becoming more and more certain there was something about Cash Mitchell that I couldn't lock out of my heart. We'd traveled together over the season, and Cash and I had talked about our time in the sport, sometimes with other teammates at dinner or just the two of us having a beer in a hotel bar after a game.

I'd heard the story about when Cash got beaned in the head by a fastball while he was at bat against University of Florida and the benches erupted into a melee. Cash told me how the other team had been trying to take Cash out to fuck up his great stats that year. He'd ended up with a concussion, but his team won the game. He'd told the story like a true warrior, not caring that he'd been injured in the process, just like so many before him.

I remembered the glowing smile on his face when he'd gone into the glory details as any ballplayer would do. "It was the top of the seventh, and we were ahead by one run. The bases were loaded..." It was a hell of a story, and I'd wanted to kiss him when he'd finished his telling of it, but that wasn't normal for a mentor with integrity, was it? I didn't think the two sides of that equation could coexist, but I'd never know if I didn't really consider the pros and cons, would I? I really fucking needed to know.

CHAPTER FOUR

CASH

"... and then, Marilee marched right up to the asshole and tossed a glass of water in his face," Keith—or Katin Blakk, his drag name—said to the group as we sat in Ben Dover's Dragtime Cabaret.

Manny then chimed in. "And see! That's what the fuck happens when they let drunk, straight dudes into the shows. Don't get me wrong, the housewives are wild, but respectful, and a diverse audience can be a lot of fun.

"Hell, the ladies generally tip well, but when they bring drunk frat boys and insecure country bumpkins who are afraid to drink a beer not opened in front of them for fear it will make them gay, shit goes to hell every time," Manuel—aka Marilee Shebangs—explained to me.

"Wait, was Uncle Skip there?" I asked, loving the stories I was hearing about my uncle's *other* life from his partner, Kimber Donlyn—whose stage name was Gimme Dong. Gimme was the emcee and featured performer at a local drag club where Uncle Skip was apparently a silent partner.

I'd come down to Miami to settle Uncle Skip's estate, and earlier in the day, Uncle Skip's lawyer, had asked me to meet him at a bank not far from the condo.

When I found the documents regarding the partnership with Kimber in Uncle Skip's safety deposit box, I nearly peed my pants laughing about how damn good Uncle Skip was at keeping his shit undercover. I wished to hell he was still alive because he could have taught me a few things.

Keith chuckled and nodded. "Yeah, Skipper was there that night. He'd been in some little Podunk town in Idaho to check out a high school pitcher for the Sharks, and when he landed in Miami, he came straight to the club because it was the night before his birthday, and he wanted to celebrate with us—his chosen family.

"So, the drunken asshole was about to beat the fuck out of Manny, and all of the queens were trying to break up the fight, failing miserably because we were all afraid of breaking a goddamn nail. Skip strolled over to the pile of bodies and grabbed the idiot by the collar of his shirt, pulling out the biggest damn gun I'd ever seen in my life and shoving the barrel up the guy's nose.

"Skipper says, 'Didn't anybody ever teach you not to hit a lady?' When he cocked the gun, the guy pissed his pants. His wife was so mad at him, she poured her drink on him before she left the club, and after the dick paid their tab, Skip walked him to the door and thanked him for coming in. I tell ya, we laughed all damn night about it. Skip just had a way about him!" Keith reminisced. I heard sniffling and turned to see Kim wiping a few tears as they slid down his cheeks.

The whole night had given me a new insight into the man I'd looked up to my whole life. What I didn't know about Skip Mitchell could fill the Grand Canyon. He was more multidimensional than I'd ever imagined he could be, and as I sat with people who loved him as much as I had, I wondered why he hadn't shared that part of his life with me. I truly wished he had. It would have been nice to know he would never hate me for who I truly was.

My other question was did the Sharks' front office know Skip was gay, and was that why they didn't do anything to honor him when he died? Had Uncle Skip shared that part of himself with the team, a part he wouldn't share with me?

I wanted those answers, but I had to figure out how to get them. Kim had insisted that he wanted to host a memorial service at the bar for Skip, and thankfully, I could surprise him with a small baggie of Uncle Skip's ashes. I had planned to sprinkle them on the pitcher's mound at Blues Stadium, so I'd think of Skip every time I was pitching a game. Under the circumstances, I believed Uncle Skip would be more at home with his friends in Miami.

The club had been closed since Uncle Skip had passed. Kim had helped me haul some family photos and a really weird coffee table Dad and Uncle Skip had made in high school back to Tampa for Mom, in accordance with Uncle Skip's will, and after we'd dropped it off, we'd spent a few days doing things around the house.

Surprisingly, Kim was damn handy, having learned how to use tools and fix all kinds of things when he worked for his father's charter business in the Keys, and he was able to help me repair the roof and fix a leaky faucet in the powder room. I could tell we were making Mom nervous because she kept pacing and wringing her hands while we were working, so after we'd checked off all the things on her "honey-do" list, we went back to Miami.

Thanksgiving was on the horizon, and Mom was planning to take a cruise with her friends, having obviously decided I had other plans for the holiday. It wouldn't be the first time I'd had a hamburger for a holiday meal.

So, there we were in the closed bar early in the morning on the Sunday before Thanksgiving week. I'd lost my cell phone in the ocean weeks ago, and I didn't really care if I ever got it back. When Kim and I had been in Tampa, he'd answered a call from Cary on my mom's landline, but he didn't get a number, and my mom didn't have caller ID.

I could have called the front office—*that* number I knew by heart—but I was pretty sure it was a courtesy call, and I needed the time for my heart to get over my crush on the man so I could make plans going forward. Getting over my feelings for Cary Brewer was my first priority.

"So, I take it you're a member of the *family*?" Keith asked as we sipped Skip's special bourbon, good ol' Jack Daniel's best.

I chuckled. "Skip's family? Yeah. He was my dad's brother," I joked, knowing what they wanted to hear, but I just couldn't say it out loud to them when I rarely ever said it to myself. One fucked-up situation at a time.

The group laughed, and then Manny sat forward in his chair with a smirk. "So, in the locker room, which one of the Blues isn't singin' *the blues*?" He wiggled his pinky finger at me, and the table erupted in laughter. It all made me smile. I'd had some fun nights out with the team, but never like I was experiencing at the moment. I felt relaxed... I felt like I *was* with family.

Kim wouldn't hear of me not spending Thanksgiving with all of the performers because it had become a tradition that they all spent the holiday together, and it had been incredibly fun. I'd talked—maybe guilted—Mom into coming down to Miami for

Christmas to see her only child, and surprisingly, the two of us had a really nice holiday staying at Uncle Skip's condo.

Mom had enjoyed meeting the queens at Ben Dover's, and they'd all adopted her as their honorary house mother. Unbeknownst to me, Mom had invited them over to Skip's condo for brunch on Christmas Eve afternoon before the show that night, and Kim had helped her cook the meal, which was delicious.

There was a Christmas Eve party at the club before it closed down until New Year's, and on Christmas Day, I'd put Mom on a plane to meet up with her friends in Puerto Rico for their New Year's celebration they'd been planning since May.

Mom had asked me to go with her, but I wanted to stay in Miami. I felt more at home with Uncle Skip's friends than I had anywhere I'd ever been.

I'd gone to the club a few times after it had reopened before Christmas, and Kim had insisted we'd have the memorial for Uncle Skip on New Year's Eve after the week off for the staff, as was tradition.

The time seemed special to Kim's memory of Uncle Skip, though Kim didn't share why, and I respected his silence. I hoped that someday, I'd have memories of a big love I'd shared with someone who would touch my soul as I could see Uncle Skip had touched Kim's.

I woke up on New Year's Eve morning and dressed in running clothes. I'd grown accustomed to running on the beautiful soft sand on the beach below the sixth-floor condo that was next door to Kim's, and I'd hate to leave it.

I'd heard the story about how he and Uncle Skip got together but lived apart. I loved the idea they had their separate spaces, but they enjoyed spending time together and were considering opening the wall between their condos to make a large penthouse. It sounded like something that could work for two independent spirits, as I guessed Skip and Kim might have been.

I ventured out into the sunny morning and stopped at the beach stairs, where I kicked off my flip-flops to run barefoot. I lit out across the sand and settled into the pace I was most comfortable with, and then I allowed my mind to wander... and it always wandered back to Cary Brewer.

I'd seen Cary's gorgeous body in the hotel shower when we were in Chicago, and all of my dreams were confirmed. As I'd suspected, he was perfect in every way I could imagine, and I wished I could have taken a picture to remind myself he was real.

Cary had a sprinkling of blond hair on his chest that spread down his sculpted abs and surrounded his thick cock like a perfectly framed picture. That treasure trail had haunted my dreams ever since that day, and I'd gone through more than one bottle of lube to get off to those mental images.

The sky was crystal clear that early morning. There was a nice breeze as I ran west on the beach toward the waves, and for the first time in a long time, I felt free. Nobody walking or shell hunting or setting up early morning sunbathing spots cared if I was gay or straight, and I wanted to feel that way every day. Unfortunately, I wanted to feel that way with Cary Brewer.

I made it the two and a half miles up the beach before I stopped and sat down in the sand. I gazed out at the Atlantic waters and thought about my life. Of course, I'd have never achieved the success I had without my Uncle Skip and his dedication to Mom and me. The things Cary had mentioned about Uncle Skip getting in touch with him about me had me intrigued. Had Uncle Skip believed Cary would be able to mentor me because I was gay, or was it because Cary was a catcher that he could bring out the best in me? Had Uncle Skip known I was gay, and if so, for how long?

I got up and dusted the sand from my shorts before I began making my way back to the condo. I had some questions for Kim, just between the two of us, and I felt like he'd keep my secret. I needed some answers before I lost my mind, so I booked it back, making a pit stop at Kim's favorite deli to get a dozen bagels so it wasn't totally awkward when I invited myself to his place for breakfast.

I took a quick shower and pulled on a T-shirt and a pair of shorts, putting the baggie of Uncle Skip in my pocket before I arranged the bagels and the container of cream cheese the server had thrown in on a tray I'd found in the cabinet. I grabbed a bottle of champagne from Uncle Skip's wine fridge and went into the hallway, knocking on Kim's door.

I was shocked when a handsome man who wasn't Kim answered the door wearing only a towel. "Oh, are you the guy from the restaurant? I, uh, hang on. Let me get my wallet," the man requested, which took me aback.

The man in the towel was probably my age, and he was quite handsome with muscles for miles and big, broad shoulders. His hair was quite short, and he had a little stubble on his handsome face, which looked really good. Then, the shock set in... What the fuck was the sexy naked man doing in Kim's apartment?

"Is Kim here?" I felt the anger rise in my body at the smirk on his face.

"*Daddy!*"

What the fuck?!

Kim came bustling into the hallway with money in his hand. He was on the phone, and when he saw me, his eyes quickly scanned my face before they glanced at the handsome man in the towel. "I'm going to need to call you back, love."

Kim ended his call and stepped into the doorway. "Come in, Cash." He then turned to the hot guy and chuckled. "You little brat! You do *not* answer the door in a goddamn towel. You'll give the girls a heart attack when they get here. Go get dressed so I can introduce you properly. Go!"

Kim stepped aside, which was when I noticed the floaty caftan he was wearing so comfortably. But the question remained—wasn't he cheating on Uncle Skip? The man had only been dead for a short time, and here Kim had already replaced Skip with a boy toy? That seemed insane to me.

I stepped inside, but I was torn about whether to stay. I hadn't called first to prompt Kim for an invite, so I couldn't really complain about his overnight guest. Hell, maybe for Kim it was time to move on? It wasn't my place to judge how long he should mourn, was it? Only Kim would know when it was time for him to get back out into the world.

"I know that platter! I told Skipper it was at his house, the jackass. Come in and get some coffee. The girls are coming over for a strategy meeting for New Year's Eve, and we're having brunch catered in. I ordered plenty, trust me. I was just on the phone with Keith, and he was picking up fruit and lox, so your bagels are right on time. Sit, sit, sit," Kim ordered with a welcoming smile.

"I don't want to interrupt. I just... My stuff can wait. I see you have your..." I completely stopped speaking as I pointed in the direction the hot guy had gone. I seriously had no idea what to say next.

"My son? He's in town for vacation, and the little shit thinks he can just show up when he wants *without any warning and mooch off me for a week*," Kim yelled. We both heard a hearty laugh from somewhere in the condo, and Kim smiled affectionately in that direction.

"Is... Is he adopted?" I knew damn well it wasn't my business to pry into Kim's personal life, but I couldn't help the question just slipping out.

Kim chuckled. "No, honey, he's my own flesh and blood. Twenty-five years ago, before I found my way into the spotlight, I worked for my father's charter service as a scuba diving instructor and shipwreck dive guide in the Keys, like I told you back in Tampa. Back then, I was an equal-opportunity cad. I identified as bisexual, and I met Keene's mother when she was on spring break with a group of girlfriends. They hired us to take them out for a dive, and after we finished the charter, I went out with the group to party. I ended up spending the night with Alisa."

"And I'm the progeny from that mistaken coupling, but neither of my parents regret it. Dad, I used the last of that fancy shampoo. I'll pick you up some more if you tell me where to find it." The handsome young guy held up a bottle and smiled at Kim affectionately, which brought a great sense of relief to me until he cast his gaze in my direction with a curious look.

"You're Cash Mitchell. We watch all the games on satellite when we're on the surface or in port. Keene Donlyn." The hot guy extended his hand for me to shake, which I did happily. I had no idea why I didn't want Kim to have someone, really, but knowing he wasn't fucking around with a young guy made me happier than I had a right to be.

"Yeah, uh, nice to meet you." My face heated at the fact he'd recognized me. It had happened before, but not very often. I'd just finished my rookie year, and I didn't expect anyone to really know about me or pick me out of a crowd, but here this guy was able to.

"Keene, are you coming by the club tonight? I have to warn the staff, or they'll treat you like a piece of meat." Kim looked at me and winked before he turned back to his son, hand on his hip as he waited for an answer.

The guy chuckled. "No, Dad. Not tonight. I'm meeting some of the guys to hang out. I'll save the fun for Skip's memorial on New Year's Eve. Oh, can I bring a date to that?" Keene then turned to me and smiled. "Are you coming?"

I felt my face flush again. "I, uh..."

"My brilliant son can drive a nuclear submarine, but he hasn't put it together yet that you and Skip have the same last name... Mitchell. Cash is Skip's nephew, Keene." Kim turned to me and rolled his eyes, which made me laugh.

Keene's handsome face turned pink, all the way up to the top of his nearly bald head. "Sorry. Sometimes I'm a little slow on the uptake on ordinary things. Anyway, it's nice to meet you. Don't let yourself get captured by 'The Four Queens,' or they'll hold you hostage all day." He then walked over and kissed Kim on the cheek, patting my shoulder as he left the condo, the slamming door signaling his grand exit.

I turned to Kim, who was bustling around the kitchen in a flutter. I chuckled, watching him. "Let me help." Of course I offered. Carole Mitchell would have my hide if I hadn't.

"If you wouldn't mind getting out plates and other stuff for the meal, I'll go change so I don't get bitched at by Keith. I'll be right back." I nodded, and Kim hurried out of the kitchen.

I went to the cabinets, which were set up exactly like Skip's, and I began pulling out plates, coffee cups, napkins, and flatware, placing it all on the counter. I remembered seeing champagne flutes on the bar in the great room, so I went to grab four, not really in the mood for a drink that morning.

I placed the bottle of champagne I'd brought from Uncle Skip's place in the refrigerator before lining everything up on the island for Kim to show me how he wanted to set the table just as the doorbell rang.

"Can you get that, honey?" I went to the door and opened it, seeing Keene standing there, red-faced.

"I forgot to get my key from my dresser. I'm worthless the first day after I put foot on dry land without one hundred thirty of my closest friends in my business. I saw the ladies pile out of a rideshare downstairs, so brace yourself, Cash." Keene chuckled.

I laughed. "I've been here since Uncle Skip passed away. I think they're trying to babysit me, which is cute. I rarely get too much time without one of them calling or dropping by. My mother was just here for Christmas, and they all had a grand old time."

The two of us laughed as I heard someone running up the stairs, knowing they were coming to see Kim since his and Uncle Skip's condos were the only ones on the top floor, though the elevator dinged a moment before the footsteps slowed down.

The *ladies,* Manuel, Keith, and Benny—the last of which I'd only met on Christmas Eve—stepped off the elevator into the beautifully appointed hallway. The style was typical South Beach art deco, and Kim made sure there were fresh flowers in the large black lacquer vase on a built-in ledge between the condo doors. The black, silver, grey, and teal color palette also reminded me that I was in Florida.

I truly loved the look of the building, inside and out, and I was looking forward to returning in the off-season, as Kim had suggested when I'd offered to sell the condo and give him the proceeds or give it to him so he could take out the walls between them and make them into a penthouse as he and Uncle Skip had planned to do.

"Are you kidding me about selling it? Do you not like the way it looks, because we—you can change it. I mean, Skip had me help him decorate, but honey, you can change anything you want," Kim suggested. We were in Skip's condo going through his things to donate, and I had Kim help me so he could pick anything he wanted to keep.

"You were his partner, Kim. You could sell it and have the money..." I began to suggest.

Of course, Kim wasn't having it. "Cash, you are the sweetest guy in the world, and someday, you're going to make someone very happy. You have Skip's generous heart, and I treasure that more than anything. I don't need money, but I will feel like the richest of men if you'll keep the place and come see an old queen when you have time."

He hugged me, and I shed a few tears. I so wished I could have known him and Uncle Skip as a couple. I'd bet my contract they'd have been like two mother hens. Hell, Uncle Skip was already that way—more so than my own mother.

I was drawn from my memory by the sight of Cary Brewer hurrying to the door of Uncle Skip's condo and pushing the doorbell incessantly. When no one answered, he began banging on the door. "*Cash! Cash Mitchell!* I know you're in there. I stopped in Tampa and talked to Carole's neighbor, and she gave me this address. *Open the goddamn door!*"

Benny, Manny, and Keith all turned to look at me as they stood outside the door of Kim's condo. I motioned for them to step inside as I stepped out, attempting to pull the door closed. When it was abruptly jerked from my hand, I saw three perfectly manicured eyebrows cocked in my direction.

I finally turned toward Cary and leaned against the wall. "You break it, you buy it."

The sexy catcher quickly swung around, and he had a wild look in his eyes. "Where the fuck have you been?"

"Right here. Mom was here for Christmas, and now she's on a cruise with her pinochle group. How about you? Where have *you* been?" I had no fucking idea what he was doing in

Miami Beach, but my insides were all topsy-turvy, and god knew the man didn't need to see me puke again.

"I've been waiting to hear from you. Usually *friends* keep in touch to wish each other Merry Christmas, but I didn't hear a word. I spoke to your mother before Thanksgiving. Didn't she tell you I called?" Cary looked hurt, and I couldn't fathom why.

"She did, but I lost my phone in the ocean, and there's no need to get a new one until I get back to Memphis. I'm sorry. The front office knew how to reach me. I gave them Skip's number here," I explained, not sure what to make of his attitude.

"Look, I plan to come back to Memphis in a few weeks, so we can get dinner or something, then. You don't have to be here for my family thing. You should go have fun. It's New Year's!" I saw Cary staring at me with an odd look on his face.

"Dinner? You wanna make a fucking *dinner* date?" Cary's question immediately embarrassed me.

"No! I mean, not a date. When I get back, we'll see each other at the stadium for the team meeting, and then we're going to Mesa for spring training. I guess I just thought you'd want time away from me because I'm sure I'm a pain in your ass. I can get one of those prepaid phones you can call if you need to check on me until I get back to Memphis." I was trying to figure out how to make the best of a clearly precarious situation.

There was whispering behind me and then a laugh. "You ready to go, babe?" Suddenly, there was a kiss to my cheek and a strong arm around my waist.

I glanced over to see Keene Donlyn standing next to me with a big smile. "What?"

"Who the fuck is this?" Cary stepped closer, definitely spoiling for a fight.

I felt Keene's arm pull me nearer, shocking the shit out of me. "Hey! You're Cary Brewer! It's nice to meet you, man. I'm a new friend of Cash's. He's my dad's neighbor, and we were just going to get brunch. You're more than welcome to join us."

I wanted to smack Keene Donlyn, but when Cary walked up to him and shoved his arm from around my waist, I wasn't sure what to do or say. "I'd like to talk with Cash in private if you don't mind."

Without waiting for a response from me, Cary pulled me over to my door and pointed at the knob. When I turned it and it opened without a key, I glanced up to see the surprise on his face.

"You always leave the door unlocked?" Cary pushed it open and walked in behind me without invitation.

"When I'm next door at my neighbor's place and not expecting company? Yeah." I was trying not to laugh at his irrational attitude.

"That's not very safe. That guy... Are you dating that guy?" Cary appeared to be really unhappy, and for the life of me, I couldn't understand why.

Of course, I panicked. My fucking career was on the line, and if he figured out I was gay? "I... I'm not dating anybody. I'm just trying to get my uncle's estate settled. He, uh, he's a silent partner in a local business that I need to decide what to do with—I mean, if I want to keep it or if I want to sell out to the partner. W-what are you doing here?"

Cary paced the foyer without responding for about fifteen seconds before he stopped in front of me and stared into my eyes, unblinking. "Are you... I'm sorry I wasn't more supportive of you after Skip died. I didn't know how much you might have needed me, or if you even wanted me around."

"Look, I enjoy my privacy. Always have and always will. I can't... There are things I just can't do. I won't give the public access to my private life. That's mine, and I won't share it with strangers." There was a defiance in his eyes that I sure as fuck didn't understand.

"I'm not..."

Cary looked at me with fire in his eyes. "I have to ask you this question because the answer is driving me crazy. The last time you were interested in someone, what was the person's name?"

Shit...

CHAPTER FIVE

CARY

I felt my cheeks heat because I knew I was bordering on crazy, but god, seeing him with that good-looking guy near his own age pissed me off more than I thought possible. I'd been telling myself I was the kid's mentor and Skip would want me to help him figure out his future... help him make decisions for his future. Skip sure as hell wouldn't want me to be attracted to his nephew, who was double-digits younger than me. *I love you like a brother, Skip, but fuck you!*

The question was out of my mouth before I could stop the words. "The last time you were interested in someone, what was the person's name?"

"I've never... That guy is Kim's son, Keene. He's currently in the Navy, but he's home on leave for the holiday. He was just aggravating me, I think." Cash was trying to explain what I'd seen earlier, but that wasn't good enough for me. He hadn't answered my question at all.

"And I'm sure he's a nice kid. You didn't answer me, Cash. The last time you were interested in anyone, who was it?" I was nothing if not persistent.

Cash stared at me for a few moments before he swallowed hard. "I've had crushes, just like anyone else. How about you?"

I could see we were going to keep dancing around the topic until one of us caved. If I wanted an answer, I was going to have to walk out on that limb by myself.

Hell, nothing ventured, nothing gained. "I'm nursing a hell of a crush right now, and I have no idea what to do about it." I thought it was an admission, but had I really admitted anything?

"Oh?"

Obviously, he wasn't going to fall for my bullshit attempt at getting him to confess anything first. When I looked into his handsome face, I couldn't speak for a moment, but then Cash smiled. "I'm gay. If you want to tell the team about it, that's fine. I didn't set out to hide it, but I learned early on that if I wanted to play baseball, I had to lie about myself." I could see the relief of his confession rolling off him.

He walked into the great room and sat down on the grey sectional, leaning forward with his elbows on his thighs as he held his head. I could tell he had stepped out of his comfort zone and admitted something he was afraid to say out loud.

If there was ever a time to support anyone, it was in that moment. I sat next to him and placed my hand on his back, absorbing his warmth through his shirt.

My heart kicked up a bit faster, and I prayed I wouldn't have a damn heart attack. "Look, Cash, I get it, and yes, I'm gay, as well. Always have been, and always will be. I'm currently fighting the most inconvenient attraction to you that I've ever had for anyone. I'm not sure what we do about it."

I moved my touch from his back, determined to keep my hands to myself, but smelling Cash's scent again was driving me crazy. What, seriously, was the worst he could do? Break my jaw? I'd gladly endure it if I got to kiss him just once.

I cleared my throat because he hadn't moved a millimeter. "What do you think we should do about this?"

Cash's head snapped up, and his eyes were terror filled. I was guessing he thought I was trying to bait him into making a move I could hold over him, so I jumped first.

"I'm going to kiss you... No, wait. I'd like to kiss you, but if you don't feel the same, break my heart, not my jaw." It was my lame-ass attempt at humor. Thankfully, Cash leaned forward and grazed his soft lips over mine before he pulled away with a cautious smile.

"I'd never do anything to hurt you, Cary. I've been in lo... I've been interested in you since I was called up from Nashville, but I thought I was being a stupid kid. I learned in college to keep my eyes and my hands to myself.

"That ended up being a lot easier to do because I was a beanpole and had nobody really interested in me. I hooked up a couple of times on apps, but nothing ever came of it." His nervous demeanor made me want to hug him tightly.

If there was a chance at something with him, I knew I had to offer him the same consideration. "I went outside the US and would contract my, uh... *companions*," I offered as delicately as possible.

I damn well didn't expect him to crack up. "Is that some hoity-toity way of saying you hired hookers?"

I laughed with him. Call it anything you wanted, but it was what it was—I was a *john*. "Hey! They were high-class escorts!" It was sort of comical.

I felt like I needed to further explain a reality to him that he might not have considered. "Catchers don't get as much notice when they're not behind the plate, so none of the pros ever recognized me, but their agencies recognized my credit card. Thankfully, they were discreet, but you need to remember you're a professional baseball pitcher and people will recognize you wherever you go. There will be paparazzi, especially during the season, so you need to become a master of disguise if you're going to go out with a guy." I hated the idea of him with another man, but it was a distinct possibility and an important point to make.

Cash smirked. "What if I'm just going out with my teammate, the best catcher in Major League Baseball?"

I chuckled. "That might work. Whew! That's a relief. So, nothing to worry about with that other guy?"

Cash stood and threw his long leg over my lap, plopping that sexy ass on my thighs as he rested his forearms on my shoulders and pushed me back against the sectional. "I'm not sure if I can keep my hands off you in public," he whispered as he leaned forward and kissed my cheek, slowly moving down to my neck. My dick was like a rod in my pants as my hands found those sweet, plump cheeks of his and scooted his long body closer.

I pulled him so his dick rubbed against mine, and then all bets were off. I wanted to fucking devour him, and it seemed as if he was totally on board with it. He had a little stubble that scraped my skin in the best fucking way, and as he nipped at my hot flesh, I felt like I was going to vanish into cinders.

He cautiously touched my cheeks with his strong hands, the callouses from the game reminding me that we were both playing with fire, and I didn't want either of us to get burned.

I pulled my head back, his hands still on my cheeks and his eyes filled with lust. "We need to talk about boundaries before we go back to your bedroom and you fuck me into the mattress." The surprise on his face was priceless.

"What?" I pressed.

"I-I... I just assumed..." he mumbled. His face flushed again —I was gonna love continuing to make that happen.

"That I was an alpha top? Nope. I prefer to bottom. Less

strain on my thighs, plus I have a hair-trigger prostate. Have you ever topped?" Something about him seemed innocent, and I had the feeling I'd freaked him out.

"Uh, no. I've never topped. I've never bottomed, either, though," Cash told me as he started to move from my lap. I was surprised, but as I thought about it, not much.

I pulled him close again. "Well, that's gonna be fun. Just to be clear, when I was with a pro, I topped. I didn't trust any of them to make myself vulnerable with them. I'm versatile, really, but I prefer to bottom with the right guy."

"Have there been a lot of *right* guys?" Cash seemed worried about my answer.

I chuckled. "One guy and one girl," I answered honestly. Cash's gorgeous face screwed up in confusion, and I laughed.

"Don't sprain your brain! I enlisted a very reputable dominatrix in Germany a few times. I'm not into pain or anything, but she was good at edging, and she was a master at pegging. I probably saw her more than anyone.

"The only guy I've bottomed for was a guy in high school. We were friends back then, and we'd played around a little. One night, we decided to fuck to see what we each liked, and I drew the short straw, so I bottomed. We didn't have lube, so he went into his house and grabbed the bacon grease his mom kept in the fridge, and for a week, I swore my farts smelled like a bacon sandwich." Cash cracked up again, and it broke the tension, just as I hoped it would. What's a little self-deprecation between friends?

I brushed the back of my hand against Cash's hard abs through his T-shirt and continued down to the front of his pants. "So, I think as long as we make sure to act like friends out in public, we should be fine. It won't be unusual to see us out together, or with other members of the team as long as we remember not to give ourselves away." I wanted to get past the ground rules so we could get to the good stuff.

"So we can do stuff together? Like go to dinner or go to a club?" Cash appeared to be excited at the prospect, and that made me happy.

"I don't know why not. I've done things with other teammates over the years. Last year, you didn't come to the cookouts at my house or any of the team dinners," I reminded him. He'd been a lone wolf most of the time, but we'd hung out a little as a group. I'd wanted him to come out with us, but I was afraid I was too obvious if I pushed him. The other guys tried to include him, but he turned down some of the invitations. That needed to change.

Cash opened his mouth as there was a knock on the door before it opened to show four guys standing in the doorway. Thankfully, that Keene guy wasn't one of them. Of course, I recognized the voice of Kim Donlyn, Skip's buddy. The other three, not so much.

"Well, well... No wonder you weren't in a hurry to come back." Kim and the other three came into Skip's—Cash's—place and closed the door. Unfortunately, Cash was still on my lap with his arms around my neck, and there wasn't really a way to explain it that wouldn't sound fake.

I placed my hands over Cash's thighs, not wanting to be indecent. "Sorry to kidnap him. We needed to discuss some things. I find it's easier to concentrate if we talk like this so I have his full attention." I always joked when I was nervous.

The four men and the one in my lap all laughed. Cash stood and pulled me up with him, walking in front of me so I had the chance to adjust my quickly deflating cock. "Cary, you remember speaking to Kim at my mom's house. This is Benny, Keith, and Manny. Guys, this is my teammate Cary Brewer."

Keith, the tall black man, gave me the up-and-down before

he smirked. "Honey, I think he plays on all of our team. Pleasure to meet you, Mr. Baseball," the man stated as he shook my hand.

The other two followed suit, but Kim pulled me in for a hug. "If you hurt him, I will break your goddamn kneecaps. Let's see you squat after that!" He pulled away with the most innocent smile I'd ever seen in my life.

I chuckled. "Nice to meet all of you. Were you friends of Skip's?"

Everyone, including Cash, snickered before Kim spoke up. "Come on over. We've been waiting for this one to come back so we could eat. Please, join us. We're planning Skip's memorial at the club."

"What club?" I asked as the man named Benny opened the door, and we all followed Kim out. Cash looked at me and winked, driving me crazy. I'd be lying if I said it didn't affect me at all.

I couldn't help taking in the gorgeous surroundings as I sat at the large dining room table in Kim's beautiful condo. Skip's place was really nice, and I'd have certainly considered it more masculine in décor, but Kim's left me speechless.

There were statues and busts on a large bookshelf, and a painting of a nude man was over the fireplace. It was Rubenesque in style, from what I remembered from art history in college, and as I looked at the face of the figure in the painting, I noticed it resembled our host more than just a little. Thankfully, a silver filmy scarf covered the guy's Johnson, so I was spared that glimpse behind the curtain if it was, indeed, Kim.

"Here, honey. Those big baseball muscles aren't going to feed themselves. So, we were talking about the feel of the memorial. Skipper had a lot of friends at the club, so I anticipate it'll be a sellout. I gave Hillary, an event planner in town, a guest list so we can keep out the riffraff. Though for there not to be some rabble-rouser in the crowd for Skip to kick out seems unnatural." Kim filled my plate with an egg casserole, crisp bacon, and silver-dollar waffles. It all looked delicious.

"So, the club? What kind of club is it?" I asked between stuffing my mouth with the delicious food. The clanging of forks dropping on the china plates was loud.

I looked up to see everyone was staring at Cash, who was chewing. When he swallowed, he took a sip of his mimosa and wiped his mouth. "I didn't tell him about Ben Dover's, yet. We hadn't gotten that far in our conversation before you came waltzing in."

Cash then turned to me. "Seems Uncle Skip co-owned a club with Kim. It's called Bend Dover's Dragtime Cabaret. It's where we're going to have the memorial."

It was my turn to drop *my* fork. "I'm guessing, based on the name, it's a gay club?" Five heads nodded. *Fucking great!*

"Duh! I'm a drag queen. We're all drag queens!" Kim looked at me as if it was obvious to the casual observer. It wasn't. Things *were* starting to make a lot of sense, though.

"So, Skip bought into a drag club? Are they really popular down here? I'm curious why he'd invest in… that kind…" It was all coming together in a surprising fashion, that was for damn sure. I looked at Kim, seeing a cocked eyebrow.

Finally, I landed the fucking plane. "You and Skip were more than business partners?"

Cash reached under the table and squeezed my thigh, alerting me I was treading on thin ice. "I'm sorry for your loss, Kim, I didn't know. Hell, he never told me he was even sick." I was backpedaling at about a hundred miles an hour.

"That's okay, honey, but you only get one stupid comment.

Next time, I bite!" I hooted with everyone else, but I definitely took him seriously. Kitten had fangs.

Cash elbowed my ribs, which hurt, but I didn't complain because for the first time ever, I was enjoying myself and *being* myself. "Okay, okay! I get it. Anyway, how long were you guys partners?"

Cash interrupted before Kim could answer. "I want to know if the Sharks knew he was gay and that's why they didn't do anything to memorialize his passing. The damn Chicago Breeze held a memorial for him." By the scowl on Kim's face, I could see it was a touchy issue.

"It sucks, not that I'd have been invited. As far as I know, it was never discussed after Skip initially told the head coach and the pitching coach at the time, who happens to be your head coach now, Dutch Weingarten. If it was an issue for Weingarten, Skip never told me." That was a surprise to me.

"How'd you guys meet, anyway?" Skip had never mentioned Kim or any of the others to me, but then again, when we spoke, we talked about Cash. Skip really didn't discuss his personal life with me or anyone, as far as I knew.

Kim stood and walked over to the fridge, grabbing two more bottles of champagne and another bottle of orange juice. "Pour us refills, Cary. This story needs alcohol," he stated. I worried that maybe I'd asked a question that was better left unanswered.

I followed orders before settling down at the table with the rest of my breakfast to listen to the story. I had a feeling Kim could craft a good tale.

"So, uh, after Keene was born, I took as many jobs as I could to help his mother, Alisa, with expenses. My parents disowned me when they found out I was gay, but Alisa has always been supportive. Oh, and she lives in California with a very nice accountant, and they have twins that are in middle school.

"Anyway, I was working at Ben Dover's as a part-time bartender when Skip came in one Tuesday night. He looked like someone had kicked his dog, so I made him a drink and gave him some snacks.

"He had a few too many that night, and I'd offered to put him in a cab, but the driver wouldn't take him unless I came along. I got the address for his apartment from his driver's license before he passed out, and I basically had to carry him up three damn flights of stairs because he was too far gone to walk.

"I slept on the couch because I was worried about him choking on his own vomit. He woke me up in the wee hours of the morning, looking all chipper. I was getting ready to storm out because he was being all kinds of cagey about a few things, but then he told me his brother..."

Cash extended his hand to Kim. "That was when Dad was killed, wasn't it?" Kim nodded, and I saw the tears, which touched me as well. After a minute, Kim got himself together and carried on.

"So, I found out that he'd lost his brother, and he had a wonderful nephew he was worried about. Skip refused to carry a cell phone back then, so it was difficult for us to stay in touch. I thought it was a lost cause, the two of us, so I started hanging out more with the queens at Ben Dover's. They took me under their wings, and then the first night I was set to perform in drag, guess who came strolling in, new cell phone in hand?" Kim stopped for dramatic effect, and we laughed, as he expected before he continued.

"Skip took me for breakfast when I got off work after closing the bar. He wanted us to talk, and we did for hours. After that, Skip became a regular at the club when he was in town and I was working. If I wasn't working, we were together.

"I became a featured performer and later the emcee at Ben Dover's on the weekends. Eventually, the sweet couple who owned the place decided to sell so they could retire, and Skip set it up for the two of us to buy it together. Now, here we are.

"Back then, I lived in a really sketchy apartment building, and Skip lived in a decent place, but it lacked personality. When this condo came up for sale, I jumped at the chance to buy it. Eventually, my neighbor decided to sell, and Skip bought that one. The night I suggested he should buy it... Ah, fond memories." Kim seemed to get lost in memories for a moment, a misty smile overtaking his face.

Then, he took his napkin and dabbed at his eyes, the smile not dimming. "Where was I? Oh! One year at Christmas, Skip returned from a scouting trip in Asia, and when he landed, he had a voicemail to report directly to the front office for a staff meeting.

"Skipper was definitely not the type of man who wanted to be ordered to do anything, so when I called to ask if he would be able to stop by the club for our Christmas party, some of the coaching staff were listening to his conversation and pissed him off. They were quizzing him about who he'd been talking to, and just to get back at them, he handed them his cell to show them a picture of the two of us at a holiday party. He basically dared them to say something about it, but as far as I know they never did.

"I have always said Skipper's 'fuck you' to the entire league, and their views on the LGBTQ community, was to buy Ben Dover's with me. Together, we made it what it is today. We've offered athletes who aren't exactly straight a place to hang with discretion, having added the VIP section upstairs and a private entrance and exit away from the street.

"Of course, there was a scandal a few years ago involving a first baseman for another team, but that's a story for another day. I still offer a port in the storm for anyone who needs it—you two will do well to remember that when you want to have fun." Kim finished his tale, and as I thought about it, it was exactly what I would have expected from Skip Mitchell.

I looked at the folks sitting around the glass-topped dining table, and I had the feeling they wouldn't out us if they were tortured with hot pokers or bamboo shoots under their nails. I pulled the sexy pitcher up with me and into my arms where I dipped him as I kissed his lips, becoming completely lost in Cash Mitchell. Hell, who wouldn't?

CHAPTER SIX

CASH

After the incredible kiss from Cary, I quickly pushed Kim to make decisions about the memorial service because I wanted to get the sexy catcher alone. No way could Cary tell me he liked to bottom and expect me *not* to explore what that meant with him.

I felt the baggie in my pocket and turned to Kim. "I, uh, I brought—saved something for you. We didn't know about you and Uncle Skip when we were in Chicago to sprinkle the ashes at Wrigley Field, but I wanted to save some for myself to sprinkle on the mound at Blues Stadium. I believe, though, that these belong to you. The ashes should have gone to you in the first place. Thank you for loving him. I wish we could have met under much better circumstances." I then handed the baggie to Kim, who held it in his hands like something sacred before he kissed my cheek and left the room with the ashes.

I looked at the others around the table to see they were all crying, and I had other things on my mind, so I wasn't going to continue to sit there when I had Cary Brewer wanting to be naked with me. "Have Kim send me a text if you need me to do anything. The service is on Thursday, so I'll be around," I told them before we left Kim's condo and went back to Skip's. I hurriedly closed the door and locked it after I had Cary inside.

"Do you need anything? Drink? Eat? Antacids?" I asked. When Cary walked over to me and took my face in his hands, I nearly died... or passed out.

"Take me to bed, Cash." *Oh god...*

CARY

My common sense told me to wait. The smart thing to do would be to give us time to get to know each other better off the field because Cash was more or less a virgin, but the side of me that was horny as fuck and wanted to get laid ignored the other asshole and took control.

"Do you have lube and condoms?" I touched that sexy body everywhere I could reach.

Cash sputtered a bit. "I-I... I didn't plan to... I don't have anything."

The sweet guy looked so forlorn, I decided to go to the emergency stash, though I was a little worried that maybe my things might have expired. I pulled my wallet from my back pocket and opened it as the doorbell rang, unwelcomed.

"*Fucking hell*! I'll get it. You don't move!" Cash pointed at me, which was cute as fuck, so I simply nodded in agreement.

I checked the date on the lube, relief flooding my system to see the stamp was damn near to infinity before I grabbed the foil packet of the condom in my wallet to see it had about two weeks until it expired. That's when yours truly did a little math. "Holy fuck. I haven't had sex in..."

"Oh, god, Kim. I love you," Cash gushed from the doorway.

There was the sound of a big smooch before the door slammed and those long legs carried his sexy ass right back to me.

"I hope you saved a few of those kisses... oomph!" I gasped as he picked me up and carried me to the bedroom, tossing me onto the king-sized bed. Cash was stronger than I actually gave him credit.

"God bless Kim. He had some things we might need. He said he doesn't need them anymore." Cash frowned for a second at the thought of what Kim meant, but then he climbed on top of me, holding up an unopened box of condoms and a new bottle of lube. I was as relieved as a teenage boy looking at a negative pregnancy test—not that it had ever really been one of my concerns.

Clothes were flying, and Cash was giggling as I skimmed my fingers up his ribs. "Stop!" he squealed, which made me laugh.

"Let's slow down a little. You're gonna learn how to prepare your partner for what I think is in your pants. You can't just slide that thing inside a guy and think he'll be okay." I pushed him onto his back, climbing on top of him to look into those soulful, whiskey-brown eyes.

I leaned forward and kissed Cash with all of the passion inside me. When the sexy man began pulling my T-shirt over my head, I slowed my movements to allow him to take control. I could see it was important to him, and hell, I didn't mind not driving the bus once in a while.

Once my shirt was off, Cash ran his calloused hands over my chest. "God, you're gorgeous. Before we do anything more, I want to be sure you know that I understand what you were saying about self-control in public. It won't be easy—trust me—but I'll be a good boy when you go out with me and people are around, I promise."

Cash Mitchell was a beautiful, beguiling young man.

There was a certain innocence about him, but at the same time, he exuded sex appeal and wonder at the same time, both of which I found very attractive. "I think that's prudent for now. I'm probably... Can we talk about this after?" I was begging, but I wanted him inside me.

The handsome pitcher chuckled. "Yeah, for sure."

After that, our tongues swirled together, and we rolled around on the bed, attempting to devour each other. We each worked to remove clothes that were in the way, and once we were both naked and lying next to each other on the bed, we took a breath, our heads facing each other.

"Your body... Damn," Cash whispered as he ran the back of his long fingers over my abs and chest.

I turned onto my side and kissed him again. He pushed me onto my back and rolled onto my body, settling between my legs as I'd hoped. Cash looked into my eyes. "What... How do I do this?"

I reached for the lube on the nightstand and sat up a bit. "Have you ever watched porn?"

"Sure, but the shit I've seen doesn't show the guy taking his time to get his partner ready for fucking. If you've got better porn, then for god's sake, show me."

I wanted to laugh at Cash's comment, but the kid was so sincere and vulnerable, I wouldn't embarrass him, so I took his hand and squeezed some lube onto his fingers before I put some on my own and lay back, propping my feet on the mattress. "First, you circle the entrance," I began, slowly circling my slick finger around my hole, gently sliding the tip inside just a bit to start things off.

Cash didn't even blink, watching me as if I were showing him the key to the universe. He gently removed my finger and worked his own around my hole tentatively, watching his motions before glancing up at me. The sensation of his touch was mind-blowing. I looked into his eyes as he began loosening me, and I was in heaven.

Cash picked it up like a pro, and he kissed me and nipped at my feverish skin as he worked his fingers into my body, nearly causing my eyes to roll back into my head. He was gentle, yet strong, and I couldn't wait to have his cock inside me. It wasn't a monster, more slender than mine, but it was long. He was cut, like me, and I wanted to take him into my body like nothing I'd ever wanted in my life. I felt a draw to him, and if we had sex, I was sure he would become my siren's song. The pitcher was a hell of a catch.

"I don't want to hurt you," Cash whispered.

I knew I needed to tell him the truth as I remembered it. "It won't really hurt. It will sting some, but I don't hate that. Get to work, *pitcher*," I joked.

Cash had already slid on the condom, and he had enough lube on it that I was afraid we'd slide off the bed, but when he inched inside me, I actually sighed in relief. It felt amazing, and in my mind's eye, I could see us fucking for years to come.

"Am I hurting you?" Cash asked.

I lifted my legs and wrapped my ankles around his waist, pulling him forward with a little force. "Not hurting, but you make me want more. Fuck me, Cash." Thank heaven, he did.

"God, Cary, it feels..."

"Harder, baby. Pound me into the..."

The sound of slapping flesh was so fucking enticing, I met him thrust for thrust, hearing Cash moan at the feel of it. I wasn't exactly the lie-there-and-take-it type, and damn, the man could fuck. I was enjoying the hell out of it.

"I'm so... I want you to come with me. Tell me how to make you come with me," Cash begged as he continued to pound into me. He was going at a pretty good pace, but I needed him to slow down just a bit. I wasn't ready for him to come yet. I was close, but I wanted to ride the wave with him.

"Slow down a little and jack me." I was begging, but fuck if I could help it. I wanted to come so much I could have cried, and with Cash sawing his long cock in and out of my body, I was so close. When his hand wrapped around my dick and began jacking me, I was ready to squeal. He leaned forward and kissed me as he continued to pump my hard rod and fuck me in a rhythm that would put most men to shame. The stamina of the young was impressive.

Cash continued to glide his fist over my dick in time with his strokes into my ass, and before I could stop it, I shot off with force, painting his hand and my chest. It was the most blissful feeling I'd ever experienced in my life. When Cash gasped and his movement into me became stuttered, I knew he'd climbed that stairway to heaven right behind me.

"*Gahh!*" The sound coming from him was beautiful. I felt his cock throb inside me. He continued to stroke me, and once he stopped thrusting, I sighed in contentment. The release of pressure was life-altering to me.

I glanced up to see sweat on his brow, but as I studied him a little closer, I saw love there, too—or maybe that was what I wanted to see. I knew I loved him, but how to tell him, given the reality in which we lived as professional sports figures, I had no idea. And what if he didn't feel the same way? I didn't even want to consider the possibility.

I went for a run the next morning... New Year's Eve... and I felt like I'd won a big prize. Cash had actually held me all night long, and the feeling touched me more than I could explain. He hadn't said he loved me, but I could feel his body exuding deep affection into mine. One day, he'd say the words, something inside me just knew it.

When I opened the door to the condo, I heard music playing, and I followed my nose to the kitchen where Cash was dancing—off rhythm—to an old love song. He hadn't even heard me come into the room, and the fact I could watch him without him knowing I was there made me feel very happy.

Unguarded moments, like what I was witnessing, were precious, and I didn't say shit like that lightly. I'd never felt that good in my skin, and based on what I was seeing as Cash sashayed his sexy ass around the kitchen, he must have been in a great mood. "What's cookin', good lookin'?" I slipped off my running shoes and tossed them into the tray by the front door.

The weather outside was gorgeous. That early morning, it was in the mid-sixties, and it reminded me what I loved about Florida. The weather in the early spring was beautiful, and the only thing that could have made my run better would be if Cash had gone with me. It was nice, though, to come back and find him cooking something for me.

"Um, French toast casserole. Kim must have come in earlier and slipped it in the fridge. I found a note on the table when I came in to start the coffee. He apologized for using his key, but it doesn't bother me. Anyway, I'm grateful he did it. I'm starved." I stepped behind him as he turned the bacon he was cooking in a large iron skillet on the stovetop, and I kissed his neck. The smell of bacon and Cash in the morning was my new favorite scent.

"Six weeks before pitchers and catchers show up. You should come run with me in the morning," I mumbled against his skin as I continued to nibble on him like he was my breakfast. I had no idea what had gotten into me, but I had to be one of the most sickening men on the earth.

Cash turned in my arms and slid his long limbs around my

neck. "That's a great idea. The time is flying by, isn't it?" He kissed the tip of my nose before he slid his lips over mine and swiped his tongue along the seam. I gladly let him in, anchoring both of my hands on his ass to hold him close as all the blood headed south again. The music faded, and another song began playing, even more sentimental than the previous one. I started laughing and pulled away from him. "What the fuck are you listening to?"

Cash walked over to an old-school boom box and popped open the cassette player. He pulled out the tape and tossed it to me. I looked at the handwritten label and laughed.

Songs for Fucking

"God only knows in what century Uncle Skip made it, but I guess he was an OG when it came to getting laid." We both cracked up at that.

"How do *you* know these songs? They're like seventies and eighties R&B. I've heard a lot of them, but you're too young," I observed as I walked over to the counter and popped the cassette back in, closing the door and hitting the Play button to continue listening.

"He always had that music playing in his old SUV when he'd come to Tampa to see us. Now I know he was probably thinking about Kim, but back then, I thought it was funny how he'd sing along. God, do you ever really know someone?" I knew he was thinking out loud, so I stepped closer to him and wrapped him in my arms before I took his hand and held it to my chest, the two of us swaying to his uncle's get-lucky playlist.

As I slowly turned us, I turned off the burner under the bacon and moved the skillet to a back burner. I checked the timer to see it had three minutes left for the casserole, so I turned off the oven and grabbed the boom box, slowly dancing the two of us back down the hallway. I wanted to see just how good that music was for fucking. I knew, firsthand, Cash Mitchell was my perfect dance partner.

Cash was finishing up in the shower, and I was sitting outside on the balcony with a towel around my waist, staring out at the beach. The way the ocean caressed the shore reminded me of the way Cash had touched me when we'd fucked the third time, me topping him. It was the first time I'd ever made love to anyone, and his first time taking me inside.

"Babe, I don't know if my ass can take another pounding," I whispered to Cash as he lay behind me, already getting hard again, the fucking stallion.

"Okay, so how long is your recovery time?" he whispered.

I chuckled. "I'm an old man—thirty-eight. It takes at least fifteen minutes, maybe twenty," I speculated as I turned and pecked his lips. The fucker flopped onto his back for a second before he sat up and climbed on top of me, flipping me onto my back. I didn't hate being manhandled, which was a new thing for me. On the ball field, I'd beat a cocky little motherfucker's ass if he crowded my home plate, but in bed with Cash, I would gladly defer to the young stud crowding me.

"How long do you think it would take if we sixty-nined and then you topped me? That give you any incentive at all?" The kid was a master negotiator. Before I knew what was happening, the kid was going down on me, and my prick was definitely rising to the occasion. He was fucking my mouth with his hard cock, but I had a better idea.

I lifted his hips to move his long rod out of my mouth, and then I pulled his ass down to settle over my face. Might as well multitask!

Within two minutes, my cock was pipe hard, and my tongue was in his ass as far as it could go. I added a finger to test him, and he didn't flinch. I felt around until I found the lube, not concentrating on the sweet licks and kisses he was giving my dick. I damn well didn't want to come in his mouth—this time. In the future, oh hell, yeah!

I lubed two fingers and replaced my tongue with them, hearing his groans of pleasure. Once I had a third finger inside his entrance, I was ready to go. "Stop and get on top of me. You can decide how quick you want to go, and if you don't like it, no problem. We can stop and go back to what we were doing," *I reminded him.*

Cash surprised me by opening the condom and popping it into his mouth before he leaned forward and swiftly went down on me, pulling back up and leaving the rubber perfectly in place. "Wow, that's a handy trick," *I joked as I put some lube in his hand. He slicked me up and got on top of me, hovering over where I was holding my dick for him to take inside.*

I looked up into his eyes and saw a little concern. "You don't have to..." *I began before he slid down my dick. A whoosh of breath grazed my skin before he froze.*

"Are you okay?"

"Yeah, just give me a second."

"Have you ever fingered yourself before?"

"Yeah, but Cary, that's not a finger jammed up there."

"Okay," *I chuckled, and when I did, his eyes glazed over for a second.* "Oh, fuck, is that... Was that my... Do that again." *It was not a request.*

I grinned at him. "We need to move so I can do what I do best." *I was bragging, but I had some moves. I held on to him and put him on his back without taking my dick out of him. His head was hanging off the end of the bed, so I dragged us back a little, holding him close to me. Those three little words almost* slipped out, but I wouldn't do him the injustice of saying I loved him while we were fucking. He deserved more of my respect than to do things half-assed.

Once we settled on the mattress, I slowly withdrew from him and slid in with a little force. The catch of his breath confirmed I'd hit my mark. "Fuck, you feel so good," I whispered as I continued my rhythm.

Cash chanted, "Yes!" "Oh, fuck!" "Again!" I felt like the fucking king as I continued to peg his prostate. I'd definitely help him find mine. I loved a good P-spot pounding, and the best I'd ever had was from Mistress Tilda, the dominatrix in Germany.

Cash wrapped his long legs around my waist, pulling me into him more forcefully, but I wasn't having it. "I don't want you to be limping tonight. I'll get you there, I swear," I told him before I pulled his ass up on my thighs and began circling my hips. He reached for his dick, but I took his hand and held it to my mouth, giving him kisses and sucking on his fingers as I looked into his eyes. I hoped he could see how much I cared about him, and I hoped what I was seeing in his eyes was confirmation he was feeling it as well.

We both blew within a minute of each other, and after I disposed of the condom, I rested my head on Cash's messy chest and hoped to fuck we became welded together—for the rest of eternity.

CHAPTER SEVEN

CASH

I stood in the bathroom, staring at the ugly striped shirt Kim had insisted I wear for the memorial. It was a thing, apparently, the eighties-style clothes. According to his friends, Uncle Skip was the king of the ugly shirt, and he had a lot of them. Kim had brought Cary and me shirts to wear, but I had a feeling maybe Cary shouldn't go.

Kim was standing in the doorway of the bathroom, smiling at us. "I'll wear it, but I'll have to wear a baseball cap and sunglasses. I don't think Cary should go. If anyone saw the two of us in the club or coming out of it, the rumors would be a problem for the Blues."

Cary was standing behind me looking at his own shirt in the mirror. It was purple, brown, and lime green. "I can't imagine where he wore this." Cary continued turning left and right to admire himself. Based on the smile, I could see he actually liked the ugly thing.

"That was Skip's favorite shirt. That style is coming back, you know. Now, about Cary coming along, I get the concern. Cash, you've got an airtight alibi why you're at a gay club because Skipper was your uncle and a partner in it. It would be disrespectful to his memory not to show—and I'd be very disappointed if you didn't come. Cary, I have an idea if you're game." Kim's reflection in the mirror showed him staring at my man with a discerning eye.

Before I knew what was happening, Cary was being whisked away, and Benny, Keith, and Manuel had me in a rideshare on the way to the club. "When will Cary be there?" I was worried about the man I loved.

"Honey, he'll be there in a little while. Don't worry. Kim is a master of disguise. It's going to be fine," Keith assured.

I was guessing I should be grateful for their assistance. I really wanted Cary to be with me because as lighthearted as the night was intended to be, I'd still be thinking of Uncle Skip, especially since I was wearing his shirt.

We arrived at Ben Dover's, and there was a line at the door an hour before the place was set to open. "How am I gonna get in? If I gotta wait, I'll get noticed, I'm sure." I knew I was whining, but it was a concern.

Manny giggled. He was a cute guy of about five-six. He was slim, and he had big brown eyes. He had a sort of pixie look about him, and his hair was cut in that fashion. My mom had cut her hair that way once, and her friend told her that the haircut wasn't for her. I'd heard about it for three months until her hair grew out again. I thought it looked okay, but I was a kid back then. What the hell did I know?

"Honey, we'll go in through the VIP entrance because right now, you own half of this dump until you decide what to do with it. Those people are on the wait list and probably won't make it inside until much later, if at all. A lot of people loved Skip. He'd come in and buy a round for everyone, especially if Kim was trying out new material that night. Skip always said he wanted his husband to be happy. If he had to buy people off, then it was money well spent," Manny confided as we got out of the car.

I was a bit surprised at the comment. "Were they married?" Manny snaked his right hand through my left arm as the two of us slowed behind Keith and Benny.

Once others were inside and the door closed, Manny turned to me and smiled. "They didn't legally marry, but I know for sure that Skip wanted to get married after it became legal. He was afraid to ask because Kim always had an 'if it ain't broke, don't try to fix it' attitude about their relationship. They had a beautiful love affair I wish you could have witnessed.

"We all knew for sure that Skip thought of you as the son he never had. I think Keene only met Skip a few times because he respected the relationship Kim had with his son and didn't want to mess with it, though I knew Skip supported Keene every step of the way.

"It was the same way Kim felt about you. I can promise, if anyone ever gives you any problems, Kim will be there with boxing gloves on. Kim didn't know you because Skip felt it was better to keep the different pieces of his life from running into each other, but Kim always called you his nephew. We all feel like we've known you for your whole life.

"Skip absolutely adored you, and he worshiped the ground Kim walked on. A few of the Sharks knew he was in a relationship with a man, but Skip said they didn't talk about it. You of all people know you do what you have to do to be able to be part of the sport you love. That's what he did. Nobody has to be a hero or a pioneer if they don't want to be," Manny continued before we went into the club, and I was whisked upstairs without a word by a waiter.

I saw the bouncers, who all waved as I was escorted to a table by the rail so I could see the stage without really being seen. Rayne, a young server wearing rainbow suspenders and a cute name tag on his chest, waited on me. He brought me a bottle of Uncle Skip's bourbon and a small, filled ice bucket with a crystal glass. He also placed another glass on the cocktail table next to it. "Oh, um, I'm here alone," I responded, certain Kim had talked Cary into staying home.

"Oh, Mr. Mitchell, nobody is ever alone here at Ben Dover's," Rayne offered with a wink before he sashayed off.

I chuckled because before Cary Brewer, an adorable guy like Rayne would have been just my type. I squirmed in my chair a little to remind myself of having Cary inside my body earlier that day. It would be a wonderful memory I'd carry with me all through my life.

The house lights went down, and the stage lights went up. I reached for my glass and plopped a couple of ice cubes inside before I uncorked the bottle of Kentucky bourbon and poured some in the glass. I placed the fifth on the table and picked up the tumbler. "Here's to you, Uncle Skip," I whispered before taking a sip.

"Buy a lady a drink?" I heard behind me. I felt a fingernail slide over the back of my neck, and a shiver raced down my spine. I stood and turned to see a tall woman in a tight blue minidress. She had long, beautiful brown hair and big blue eyes. Her nails were long and red, talons like I'd never seen. She kept staring at me, and I felt like I was sixteen again, trying to deal with the head cheerleader who wanted to date me. I was as flustered as I'd been back then.

The woman walked around the couch and sat down without invitation. I started to protest, but Kim walked on stage and the music stopped. "Ugh," I heard my companion groan, her voice much deeper and louder than it had been when she approached me. She reached for her glass and held it out to me. "Two cubes, please, handsome. The fucking things I do for you..."

I turned to really take her in, and I saw a cocky smile I recognized. "Are you fucking kidding me?"

"*Happy New Year!* Welcome to Ben Dover's Dragtime Cabaret! I'm your hostess tonight, Gimme Dong," Kim introduced to lots of laughter and a standing ovation as I pulled a very sexy Cary—in drag—closer and tucked him in front of me so I could whisper over his shoulder. The crowd was going wild over Kim's introduction.

"How in the hell did Kim talk you into this?" I whispered as I leaned forward and blew in his ear to taunt him. Cary elbowed me in the side and jiggled his glass, so I fixed him a drink and handed it over, picking up my tumbler to hold in front of him.

"Happy New Year," I toasted before I kissed his cheek, feeling it smooth as silk. "You shaved?" I asked.

Cary laughed. "I shaved *and* I tucked. You owe me bigtime." We both laughed and turned back to the stage.

Kim was standing in the middle of the spotlight with a forced smile. His drag persona was wearing a black sequined gown and a red wig. The makeup was flawless, just as Cary's was, and I would have to give credit—Kim was a hell of a showman... showwoman... showperson? He had a hell of a talent.

"Under ordinary circumstances, I'd be singing my fat ass off—or, you know, moving my lips to a recording of some fabulous diva so I could take your money to pay for more lipstick," Kim joked. The audience laughed. I heard it, but my eyes were fixed on Cary.

"Is it... Why would you do this?" I couldn't begin to imagine the trouble he'd gone to for me.

Cary sipped his drink and turned to me. "Because, not unlike Skip Mitchell, I find I'd do anything for you. We were worried about someone spotting us together, so this way, if anyone happens to see us, it's just you with your date at your uncle's memorial service wearing that ugly fucking shirt." Cary leaned forward and kissed my cheek. He then reached up and smudged his thumb over it, showing me red lipstick. I wanted to laugh, but then Kim began to speak.

"We all knew and loved Skip Mitchell. As some of you might have heard, Skipper had pancreatic cancer and left us just before Thanksgiving, which is why we've been closed. Tonight, we're going to give Skip a Ben Dover's send-off." You could have heard a pin drop for a moment before the crowd stood and applauded.

Cary and I looked down to see Kim with a big smile on his face as he gently dabbed his eyes with a handkerchief that matched his black dress. "Fuck, I forgot to ask if this shit is waterproof," Cary whispered as he reached up and nearly poked out his eye with a long red fingernail while trying to wipe at the corner of his eye where a tear slipped free. I grabbed a napkin from the tray on the table and dabbed at it before I kissed his cheek. He was quite a prize, and I owed Uncle Skip a debt for bringing Cary Brewer into my life without me even knowing.

I took his hand, and we both stood, walking over to the railing to get a better look at the stage. I pulled Cary in front of me and kissed his neck as we stood there together. I snaked my arm around Cary's waist, pushing my hard dick into his ass.

"Maybe I'm not gay? I'm really fucking attracted to you right now." I'd once read that many people had an innate need to feel alive after losing someone they loved. Me wanting to strip Cary naked and have him fuck me right there could have been a manifestation of that desire. However, it didn't make sense that I was so attracted to Cary as a man, and now, supremely attracted to him dressed as a woman. I was confused as fuck.

Cary turned to look at me and took my hands. "You're still

gay, baby. It's just seeing me in a different light. Next time we visit Kim, I'm gonna have him give you a makeover. Oh, and I have a surprise. Wait until you see how good my ass looks in the garter and the thigh-highs. I get to keep those, by the way." Cary leaned forward and kissed me gently.

"So, this evening is dedicated to Stephen Skip Mitchell. Our friend, our supporter, and my personal hero and the love of my life. All of the tips and profits from the bar are going to the hospice organization that took care of Skip in his last days." Kim nodded, and the music cranked up. One of the queens came out, and the performances began.

The cute twink waiter stepped over to me and touched my shoulder. "You have a visitor. May I seat them at your table?" Rayne asked. I turned to see Keene Donlyn with a beautiful young woman holding his hand.

I turned to Rayne. "Sure. Bring them whatever they want to drink and put it on my tab. Thanks, Rayne." I then turned to my date. "You okay, sweetheart?" I asked, feeling his tight body shake a little as he laughed quietly so as not to give himself away.

Cary turned and whispered, "I'll make you pay if you torture me with this later." I patted his ass through the dress and led him over to the curved couch, helping Cary sit down as I finally looked at the black stockings and black pumps he was wearing. They were really fucking huge. "Whose shoes?"

"Keith's. That guy has huge fucking feet. Kim stuffed cotton balls in those pointy toes, so they don't hurt too much. They're way too fucking big." Cary totally made me laugh with his complaints.

I then turned to our new companion. "Keene, man, good to see you. This is my friend Cary." I didn't say anything beyond that, and Cary pinched my ass, making me laugh. Cary stuck out his hand to shake, and when Keene took it, three fake red nails popped off.

"Oh, shit! I'm so sorry!" Keene picked them up and handed them to Cary, which was really kind. The moment was heavy with embarrassment on both of their parts, but Keene's date elbowed him, nearly knocking him down.

Keene looked at her and grinned. "Cary, Cash, this is my friend Stephanie." The young woman smiled and extended her hand to us, and I was gentle with it, seeing her nails were long and red as well. She was a beautiful blonde, and she had some killer curves, which I could see Keene seemed to like as he held her tight against his side.

Rayne brought them a bottle of wine and two glasses, and we all turned back to the show to see all of the queens who worked at Ben Dover's had taken a turn performing that night were bowing and making curtain calls. They circulated through the crowd, collecting tips from the patrons who offered them. It was a pretty jovial crowd, and I was grateful so many people wanted to honor Uncle Skip.

Rayne came to check on us, and Cary leaned into me. "Give him a hundred dollars to donate to the cause, will you? I'll pay you back," Cary whispered.

I reached in my back pocket and pulled out my wallet, removing two hundred dollars, before I motioned for Rayne to come over. "Can you give this to Gimme and ask her to split it with the others? Tell her I'm donating to the hospice organization independently, but I want the queens to have a drink on me and Cary." The young man nodded, and as he was walking away, Keene reached out with a hundred of his own. I was sure Kim would be proud of his son.

The performers went on break for thirty minutes before the eleven-o'clock show that would count down the new year. "I need the little girls' room. You wanna go with me, Cary?"

Stephanie had a nice smile as she held out her hand. I'd noticed Cary had only been sipping his drink, and I was guessing he didn't want to have to untuck and retuck in a public bathroom.

"I think I know what's wrong, and I promise I can help you, Sweets," Stephanie offered.

"Hell yeah! I'll go with you." Cary stood to leave without looking around, so I stood and offered a hand to steady him before Stephanie took his arm.

"It takes a little time to adjust to everything, I know, but you're doing just fine. Where are you in the process?"

I quickly looked at Keene to see he was watching them walk away with a big smile. "She's beautiful, isn't she? I met her last time I was here to visit Dad, and I ran into her the other day at the coffee shop where she works as a barista. She took her break, and we sat and talked for a while. When she got off work, I was waiting for her and took her for dinner. I totally blew off the guys, and I'm sure I'll hear about it when I get back to base, but I don't care." As I looked at him, I could tell he wasn't lying. He really liked Stephanie. I was completely worried that Keene wasn't seeing the whole picture.

"She seems really nice. I'm not sure about..." I had no idea how to express my thoughts without pissing him off, but I felt like he needed to know for both of their sakes.

"Stephanie will help your friend. She's a year post-op, and she's very open with discussing her transition. She's an activist, and she's also been in your friend's position, so they're in good hands." Keene gave me a look of assurance and a kind smile of support.

I, however, couldn't imagine he didn't recognize Cary! Maybe he did and wasn't about to pass judgment on anyone? I seriously had no idea what to say.

A few minutes later, Cary and Stephanie came back upstairs, both of them smiling and chatting. I noticed Cary didn't seem to be upset, and I was relieved. "Everything okay?" I offered my hand to help Cary sit down on the couch next to me, and when he kissed my cheek and crossed his legs without groaning, I was definitely relieved.

Cary leaned close to me. "I've got a bone to pick with Kim, the bastard—*pun intended*. He had me trussed so damn tight I thought I'd break my dick." Cary then tossed the long brown hair over his shoulder, exposing his neck to me. I was just fine with that, especially when a familiar song began to play over the sound system. It was one of the songs from the cassette tape I'd found at Skip's home.

When people got up and started dancing, I turned to Cary. "Can you dance in those shoes?" He smirked, and I noticed his lipstick was perfect, once again.

"Better than you can dance without them." We both laughed, and I took his hand and turned to Keene.

"We're going to dance. We'll be back. If you want something, order it. I've got the tab, Sailor." The young man chuckled and nodded, and I took Cary's hand and pulled it through my arm so he could lean against me as we traversed the stairs to the main floor.

Once we arrived downstairs, we made our way through the crowd to the dance floor just as a new song came on—one of Uncle Skip's favorites since it was on the tape twice. *Let's Stay Together* by Marvin Gaye started to play, and as I took Cary in my arms, I knew it to be truer than anything I'd ever believed in my life.

"I can't believe you let Kim dress you up like the most beautiful woman I've ever dreamed of just so you could be here with me tonight. You're incredible, Cary," I whispered as I pulled him closer. He was taller than me with those high heels, but I was at just the right angle to kiss and suck on his neck... and I did, happily.

We danced, and I kissed Cary the whole time through that song and the next. Ten minutes later, Cary accepted a dance with an older gentleman familiar to all of the queens, so I asked Kim to dance. The songs were so familiar, I had to laugh. "So, this is Uncle Skip's fucking playlist?"

Kim laughed, his deep voice making me smile as we swayed around the floor. "He loved this music. He'd turn on that damn playlist... Well, when I got off the elevator and heard that music, I knew I was in for a good night.

"Skipper was always intentional in everything he did—as in he never hid his feelings from me. He told me he loved me, and he showed me every day. I want the tape back that I left in the boom box, but I burned you a CD. That tape has sentimental value to me. Do you mind?" Kim asked.

I chuckled. "No, but those songs now have sentimental value to me as well."

Kim laughed. "It's addicting, isn't it? Love, I mean. Those feelings are so incredible, and I know I'll miss them. Part of the grief process is accepting that there's no one out there who waits for your call or laughs at your jokes anymore.

"There will never be anybody who will yell at me for leaving on the bathroom light at my place instead of coming over to sleep with him when I get home from a long night at the club. I'm afraid of the dark, you see, for reasons that are too melancholy to discuss. I just couldn't wake him when I got home so late, but I still knew he loved me whether I was in his bed or he was in mine. We were making plans for changes before he got sick.

"That's why I envy you, Cash. Cary loves you like Skip loved me. That very alpha man let me put him through the mill to change his look so he could be here with you tonight to support you in this loss. That's the sign of a keeper, sweetheart."

If I didn't already know it, he'd made a compelling argument.

"Yeah, you're right. So, any advice for a newbie?" I asked as we slowly danced around the parquet floor.

"A newbie at what?" Kim wore a kind smile before he chuckled as if he knew what the hell I meant. The man was damn smart.

"A newbie at love? How the hell do you even do it?"

The lights flashed, and Kim checked his watch. "Honey, you are in for the ride of your life, especially since you're both professional athletes. Please, be careful. Skip told me once that he loved his job but hated it in equal measure, because it kept us from being together in public. I won't lie. At times, it put a strain on our relationship because we couldn't be 'us' outside of these four walls, really.

"This club, it's like a safe harbor for people who come here. Most of them are looking for a place to be themselves away from the prying eyes of the judgmental public, even if they're not celebrities like you and Cary. The pressure on the two of you must be tough, so remember you always have a place to be yourselves. I feel like you're my nephew, or even my son. I only want the best for you, Cash." His words touched me such that I leaned forward and kissed his cheek.

"Can I buy that outfit from you?" I teased as I pointed to where Cary was dancing with Keith. I laughed at the two of them dancing together, both in drag, but they seemed to be getting along, so I was grateful.

Kim giggled. "It's a gift from me to him. He seemed rather taken with it. You two enjoy each other!"

On New Year's morning, I awoke with a hell of a headache. I was resting my head on Cary's shoulder, and I saw his lipstick was smeared and his wig was on the floor, but he had a sweet smile on his face which made me grin.

I went to the bathroom, and when I pushed down my boxers to pee, I saw red smears on my dick, reminding me of what had happened the previous night.

I chuckled as I finished my business and turned on the shower to allow it to heat up. Cary and I were heading back to Memphis that day before we were required to go to Arizona for spring training. I had Cary's dress and the sexy lingerie that accompanied it in my luggage because that outfit had driven me wild. Seeing the ensemble when I peeled that dress off Cary had me salivating to suck his cock, while he wore the stockings and the garter belt. If he'd really enjoyed it, I'd buy those things in every color he liked.

I walked down the hallway to the kitchen and turned on the Keurig for coffee. When I went back to the bedroom, I noticed Cary was sitting up against the headboard, trying to wake up.

"I turned on the shower, but would you rather take a soak? Uncle Skip has that big tub," I suggested.

He'd sucked my dick, and then I'd sucked him off, followed up by Cary fucking me hard, both of us wound up by the way he'd looked at the club. A soak sounded like a good idea to me.

We were set to leave in a few hours to drive back to Memphis in Cary's SUV, and I really was ready to get home. I needed to set a schedule to begin regular workouts at Blues Stadium so I could tune up a little for the upcoming season. I'd promised Cary we'd get together to work out, so at least I could see him regularly. What happened when we returned home, I didn't know, and it was worrying the fuck out of me.

"Did you turn on the coffee maker? I could take a soak," Cary agreed.

"I did, as a matter of fact. Why don't you wash your face and get in the tub while I get us some coffee? We should get on the road in a couple of hours, right? That's what you said last night."

Cary reached for me and pulled me down with him onto the bed. "I had fun last night. How about you? Did it freak you out to see me like that?"

I laughed as I kissed his lipstick-stained mouth again. I was still overwhelmed he'd gone to all of that trouble for me, and I'd never forget it. "No. I think I showed you how turned on I was when we got home this morning and I sucked your cock in the kitchen when we got a drink of water.

"Thank you for agreeing to something so crazy, Cary. I can't tell you how much I appreciate the fact you were there to show your respect to Uncle Skip and support me. I lo... I appreciate everything you did." Thankfully, I caught myself before I fucked up and declared my undying love to a man who probably didn't want it.

Cary placed both of his hands on my face, his thumbs caressing my cheeks. "I wanted to be there to support you as much as I could, Cash. It was fun, though. I had no idea I looked so damn sexy in drag.

"Now, I hate the fact we can't make love again before we go back to reality, but we'll figure everything out, I promise you. I can't imagine going through the entire fucking season without being able to spend time with you." Hearing Cary's declaration made my day.

How to make that hope a reality? Well, that remained to be seen, didn't it?

CHAPTER EIGHT

CARY

I slowly walked off the field to head down the tunnel that led to the locker room at the practice venue we were using in Mesa. I'd been assigned to a two-bedroom apartment at the Extended Stay Residential Inn where the team had taken over for spring training.

The place definitely wasn't four stars, but it was the best the city of Mesa, Arizona, had to offer to an MLB team, so there we were. I was sharing an apartment with a new catcher, Rico Suarez, a nice guy who played for the Nashville Blue Notes and had been recruited right out of high school. From what I'd deduced, he was a decent kid, but he seemed scared as fuck when I tried to talk to him.

Cash hadn't been so lucky. He was sharing with a Triple-A pitcher he wasn't fond of at all. Dutch Weingarten, the head coach, had decided in the off-season that he wanted more strength in the bullpen, so he and Lou Clayton, the bullpen coach, had decided to assign us to share apartments with the farm team players to support the younger kids. I wasn't happy about it, either, but some shit was out of our control.

When Cash and I had talked on the phone at night, he'd bitched about the living arrangements for the first hour. I really didn't give a damn about anything other than hearing his voice and hoping the two weeks we had to be there would go by fast.

We were returning to Memphis for a week before the whole team had to report back to Mesa, and then the roommate situation would fix itself. Cash and I would share because we were starters, and we'd shared the previous year.

"*Brewer!*" The sound of my name being called echoed off the bleachers of the stadium we were using at the junior college in Mesa. It was a football stadium, but we were using it for practice since the college had phased out their football team. I was guessing the rent the team paid was propping up the school, but it wasn't my concern at the moment.

I stopped and turned to see Cash jogging toward me, and I stifled a grin. My man had been suffering a pitching slump, and I knew him well enough to know he was freaking out about it. He was working with a new catcher who hadn't solidly picked up the pitching signals, and I was sure he was about at the end of his fuse with the guy.

"Hey, Mitchell. What's up, kid?" I asked as the other pitchers and catchers headed toward the locker room.

"Kid, *really?*" Cash asked. I could tell he was agitated, and as I looked around, I was grateful to see no one had really noticed the two of us standing at the entrance of the tunnel.

"Sorry, Mitchell. What can I do you for?" I took in his tense appearance, and I didn't like it at all.

Cash chuckled. "I'll give you anything I have, all day long, if you'll do me. Anyway, how about we take out our roommates for dinner before I wrap my fingers around the asshole's neck and end him? Are you available?"

"Sounds good. Any particular reason you want to kill your roommate?" I wanted any reason to spend time with him, even if I had to deal with his dickhead of a roommate at the same time.

"Nick Gregson is driving me up the fucking wall. He was a coddled high school pitcher—All District and All State in his little one-horse hometown. He got a spot on the Blue Notes right out of high school, and he knows no humility. I'm trying my damnedest not to strangle him in his sleep. He has this clicking thing he does at night that I can hear through my closed bedroom door, and I'm ready to start sleeping in the goddamn bathtub so I can have another barrier between us.

"I've tried to get to know him, but he's a goddamn jock, and I hate jocks." My sweet Cash was whining, which I thought was kinda cute.

I leaned against the wall of the tunnel and crossed my ankles. "Somebody needs to get laid. It's only two weeks."

Cash nodded. "Yeah, but my situation has nothing to do with my personal wants or needs. I'm telling you, the kid is an asshole, and he's reckless. We had an hour-long discussion this morning about how much damage could be done by throwing a curveball to bean a batter. He put a rival team's first baseman in the hospital with a concussion and a broken jaw, and he's fucking proud of it, the asshole. The guy's a goddamn psycho."

I didn't like the idea of anyone purposely hurting a batter. The fact he'd done it and put someone in the hospital had me worried. "Yeah, let's get dinner tonight. I wanna know more about this jackass." Cash nodded and popped me on the shoulder with his glove as he headed into the locker room.

Goddamn if I didn't want to push the man against the cinder block wall and kiss him, but I knew it was against the rules we'd agreed to on the drive back to Memphis from Miami.

How much did I want to say fuck the rules?

When I headed into the locker room, the music was loud, per usual. Classic rock was blaring over the speakers, and the guys were in various modes of undress. There was only one guy I wanted to see naked, and his locker was in the row behind mine, so I ignored everyone else.

I ambled over to my locker and sat down to take off my cleats. I pulled off my practice shirt and tossed my dirty clothes into my duffel. I'd need to do laundry soon or the fucking stench would make it impossible for me to sleep in my own room. Maybe I'd ask Cash if he wanted to meet in the laundry room of the building to wash clothes and make out? Sounded like a good idea.

"Brewer, man, when the fuck are you gonna retire and give some of the rest of these kids a chance?" The voice was coming from my left, so I turned to see a familiar face. It was Jeff Quattlebaum, a guy I used to catch for at Ann Arbor before he dropped out his junior year to take a walk-on tryout with a Canadian MLB team, the Windsor Rebels.

From what I'd heard, Jeff had made the team, and I hadn't seen him in probably fifteen years. He got sent down to the Rebels' farm team because of a rumored drug problem, so seeing him in the locker room was a surprise.

I stepped over to him, extending my hand to shake his. Something about the way he looked at me had me uneasy, but I plastered on a fake smile and offered, "Jeff! You son of a bitch! How the hell are you? What brings you here, man?" I crossed my arms over my chest to study him because I knew there was an ulterior motive behind his visit.

Jeff had been a jock back when I knew him in college, and I remembered him as the most reprehensible asshole I'd ever met. Most of the girls I knew from back then hated the fucker, saying he was aggressive and disrespectful to them. From what I could recall, the jackass had a lot of first dates at Ann Arbor, and I was sure more than one restraining order against him.

"I'm a sports agent now, Brewer. I guess you haven't heard,

but I got Pedro Arenas signed with the LA Stars, and I have another deal in the works.

"I talked to Roger Hardy over the holidays about what the Blues need. We were both in Aspen for Christmas, and I was telling him about a kid outta Texas I found last fall. He's ready to go to the show right now!" He seemed more than a little excited, which had me worried.

"What position?" I asked, dreading the answer.

"He's a pitcher—southpaw—which Roger said he really needs. This kid can throw a hundred-mile-an-hour fastball, and his fucking changeup is a thing of beauty."

Jeff then stepped closer. "Roger said he wants to dump Mitchell, so he wants my guy to try out on Wednesday when Dutch and Sandy are here to take a look. Ironically, Mitchell is staying in the same suite as my kid.

"I want you to warm up my pitcher and pump up his confidence. You remember being that eighteen-year-old kid when we were at Michigan, right? You're the best catcher in the league right now, Brew. Will you do it?" Jeff asked.

My gut was churning, but not because the son of a bitch asked me to help his kid at the tryout. Hearing him say Roger was actively trying to get rid of Cash had been like a slap in the face, and hearing it was Cash's roommate that Jeff was pushing made me sick. That shit wasn't going to fly in the least.

Later that night, Cash and I took our roommates to dinner at a well-reviewed steak house in University Hills, not far from the stadium where we were training. We'd taken a cab from the hotel, and I hadn't had time to talk to Cash before, but I planned to get him alone at least for a few minutes to kiss him after.

I paid the taxi fare for us, and we all went inside. I pulled on the back of Cash's knit shirt to stop him, and after the other two idiots went inside without looking back, I let go of the shirt and smiled at my man. "Say, isn't that my shirt?" I joked, seeing my blue polo shirt that I knew Cash had cabbaged onto in Miami.

"I don't know what you're talking about. I found this lovely shirt in my suitcase when I got home. It still smells nice," Cash gloated as he winked at me.

"Fine, but your wardrobe is now available to me when we get back to Memphis. I need to do laundry tonight after we eat and dump those two dickheads. Do you have some laundry to do? I really need to talk to you," I explained as the two of us slowly made our way to the front door.

Cash opened it, and as I walked by, he sniffed me. "Goddamn, you smell great. Yeah, I'll meet you down there at nine. Curfew is at ten, so can we discuss your issue in an hour?"

"And mutual hand jobs? You bet. Now, get the asshole to talk, will ya?" Cash nodded, and we went inside.

After the four of us were seated, we all perused the extensive menu. I glanced at Cash, seeing his brow furrowed in concentration. Damn if he didn't look sexy as fuck. "Mitchell, you wanna share a bottle of wine, or are you having beer?" I asked.

Rico was eighteen, and the kid was a fucking rock star on the field. The asshole with Cash, Nick Gregson, pissed me off just to look at him. "I'll have a whiskey neat. Wine is for faggots," Gregson offered as he slouched in the chair like a fucking delinquent who thought he knew every fucking thing. I hated guys like that.

I glanced at Cash to see his cocked "I told you so" eyebrow. I gave him a subtle nod and opened the wine menu, before I slammed it closed and leaned forward in my chair to address the little fucker.

"First off, I'll beat you to within an inch of your life if you ever say that word in front of me again. So, where are you from, Gregson?" I asked, sitting back a little and resting my forearms on the table. Unfortunately, Cash was sitting across from Rico, so I couldn't touch him, which aggravated me.

Of course, the little bastard, who was just a bit younger than Cash, sat forward to challenge me from his seat across the table. "Ring a little too close to home for you?"

I started to get up when the server approached. She was a girl of about twenty, and if that stupid dick across from me made a rude comment, I would lead him out of there by his ear and beat his ass in the parking lot.

"Good evening, gentlemen. I'm Tasha, and I'll be your server. You're Cash Mitchell and Cary Brewer, right? I've got a five-dollar bet with the bartender that I'm right," she informed with a sweet smile.

"Yes, ma'am. You tell the bartender to pay up. Any specials?" Cash asked with a smirk. The server listed off various steak sizes and prices, and when I glanced up, I could see Gregson was pissed that the young woman didn't know *his* name.

After she finished, I ordered a bottle of shiraz for Cash and me, remembering it was one he liked when we'd gone out to dinner with the queens from Ben Dover's the night before we left town. Rico ordered a cherry cola, and when I saw Gregson open his mouth, I sat up and looked at the young lady. "He'll have a cola, too. He's in training. Oh, can we get an order of the calf fries?" I asked.

The young woman stopped typing into her tablet. "You know what they…" Tasha attempted to caution. I chuckled and glanced at Cash to see he was a little confused.

"Yes, and can we get an order of the crab cakes as well?" Tasha nodded and left the table. A minute later, water and warm rolls were delivered to the table.

After the male server left us, I turned to Gregson. "So, where'd you go to college?" I asked.

"University of Texas. You?" The kid was challenging me, and I hated to tell him that he wasn't a worthy opponent.

"University of Michigan. How did your teammates at UT not beat the fuck outta you?" Gregson was an asshole, and I didn't suffer assholes.

"*Ow!*" Rico exclaimed. I turned to see Cash with a strange look on his face as Rico slid back his chair, rubbing his shin. I wanted to laugh my ass off.

"S-sorry, Rico. I was trying to cross my legs. So where did *you* grow up?" Cash tried to cover, but it made me chuckle.

The conversation jumped off from there, but Nick Gregson kept his mouth shut and continued staring daggers in my direction. I could tell he was seething, but he was smart enough to pick up that I was taking in his every move, so he didn't react. I didn't know, and I damn well didn't care, what he thought of me.

When the calf-fries came with a horseradish cream dipping sauce, I pushed the plate toward Gregson. "Try 'em. They're great," I challenged. I picked up one, having tried them once on a dare. The joke was on my teammates—I didn't hate them, even after I found out that they were calf nuts.

Gregson picked one up and smelled it before he dipped the thin-sliced fry in the sauce and bit into it. Cash reached for one, but I slapped his hand. "You won't like them."

Gregson shrugged a little and proceeded to dive into the calf fries, hoarding them from the others. The other three of us shared the crab cakes and chatted with Rico about his family. "I've got three younger brothers and one little sister. If I ever got the chance to play in the Bigs, I could help my parents put them through school when the time comes. I wasn't book smart like the rest of the kids, and if any of them have a chance to go to college, I want to make sure that happens." I liked his answer a whole lot.

I poured Cash and myself each a glass of wine and watched Gregson finish with the appetizer without offering to share. That was fine with me. Once he was finished, he pushed away the empty plate. "Those were really good. Never had them before."

I took a sip of wine and put my glass on the table, glancing in Cash's direction to see he was aggravated. I winked at him before I turned to Gregson. "That's really surprising, considering you went to school in Texas. Lots of beef down there."

Gregson took a sip of his soda and sat forward. "I'm not from Texas, originally. I grew up in L.A. My family moved to Texas after I got into UT."

I nodded. "Yeah, probably not a lot of restaurants serve calf nuts, huh?"

"Wh—wh—what?" The kid's face was white as a sheet.

"Calf nuts. When they castrate bull calves, they keep the nuts and slice 'em up and batter them. Looks like you liked them a lot," I added as I pointed to the empty plate.

If the guy could run the bases as fast as he ran to the bathroom, it would be a shame not to have him on the Blues, but I couldn't stand the bastard. Cash's chuckle caught my attention. I glanced up and saw the smirk on his face, and then the three of us started laughing.

After dinner, I got us a cab back to the hotel. We took the elevator up together, and as we stood in the back, Cash retrieved his phone, pecking quickly into the screen before he put it away. My phone vibrated in my pocket as the elevator stopped on their floor.

We all said good night, and when the doors closed, I retrieved my device and saw the text from Cash.

I'll meet you in the laundry room. No boxers. I don't want anything getting in my way.

I sent back a kiss emoji just as the elevator stopped on the third floor. Rico and I got off, and he let us into the suite. After I closed the door, I went into the living room and placed my wallet and phone on the counter.

"Rico, I'm going to go do laundry. You need me to throw in a load for you?" I had no idea why I suddenly felt cordial. It had to be the excitement of getting to put my hands all over Cash, but maybe the kid could benefit from Cary Brewer being happy for a while?

"Really? You don't mind, Cary?" The kid looked surprised at my offer. I shook my head, and Rico was off like a shot. He came back with a trash bag full of laundry, and I looked at him, seeing his tanned cheeks turn pink.

"I didn't have a chance to do it before I came down. I had a few clean things, but, uh..." I could see he was embarrassed, so I laughed.

"Don't worry about it. We've all been there. Any particular sorting?" If he was particular about the way he did his laundry, it would buy me a little more time with Cash, so I didn't mind it much.

"Nope. I've been doing my own laundry since I was thirteen. All my shit is grey." Rico was joking, but it struck a chord with me. As he reached into his pocket and pulled out his wallet, I waved him off.

"I got it." I hurried to my room, changing into sweats—no boxers—and a T-shirt before I grabbed my dirty things, dumping them into the bathroom trash bag as Rico had done.

I went back into the common room, hiding a far-too-happy

grin. "If a beer or a bottle of liquor from the minibar happened to go missing, I wouldn't tell anyone."

I gave the kid a wink and hustled out to the hallway. Rico seemed like a good kid, and one beer wouldn't hurt him.

I rushed down the stairs to avoid the slow-as-fuck elevator—and that idiot, Gregson, if he decided to go out again—and I skidded into the laundry room to find it empty.

I quickly dumped the kid's laundry into the machine and shoved in ten quarters along with a small box of detergent and a single serve of fabric softener that was in a nice basket on the folding table. When I heard the elevator ding, I walked into the hallway in time to see my man step off with a pillowcase filled with clothes.

"Well, well! Look who it is? The star pitcher of the Memphis Blues! How lucky am I to find you in the laundry room... all alone... looking sexy as hell?" I couldn't help myself. I'd missed him.

Cash laughed. "Only one machine?"

I nodded.

"You already have a load in?"

I nodded again before I snickered and responded. "I'd like to, but no, that's the kid's clothes. I thought I'd buy myself some extra time. We can throw ours in together. You wear my clothes, too. Guess they can be washed together."

Cash dropped his bag and pushed me into the small bathroom, closing the door. "You listen to the washer. I've got better things to do." When he pulled down my sweats and hit his knees, I damn well didn't argue.

I'd fucking missed his hot mouth, and as much as I wanted to go down on him at the same time, I wasn't about to lie down on the fucking floor of the bathroom so we could sixty-nine.

I fucked his beautiful face until he swallowed me into his throat, and then I couldn't hold back. "Mmm... Give it to me!"

And I did. Cash gasped between shots of my come nearly choking him.

He gulped down what I gave him until I had nothing left. I backed away and helped him from his knees, kissing him with everything inside me. I stopped the kiss and nuzzled into his neck as the washer buzzed.

"God, that felt so good, baby. Stay here. I'll go move the kid's laundry and put ours in. I'll be back." When I walked out into the laundry room, I saw the door to the hallway was open.

I thought Cash closed it, but maybe I was wrong? I quickly changed out the laundry, counting out two dollars' worth of change and shoving it into the dryer and then putting another two-fifty into the washer before I went back to the bathroom and closed the door.

I locked it, just in case, and I turned to take in the beautiful sight of Cash slowly stroking himself. I could see he was close to blowing, but I wanted to make it good for him, so I took his hand and kissed it. "God, this is the slowest two weeks of my fucking life." I had something more important on my mind than that shit with fucking Jeff Quattlebaum in the locker room earlier in the day. I had something I wanted desperately, but how to get it? Good question.

"Yeah, you can say that again. Look, I wanted to ask if maybe you'd think about moving in together back in Memphis? I know it could be a little harder to do, but I think we can explain it away. We can get a bigger place together, ya know?"

I had a great house in Memphis, but if Cash would consent to live with me, then I'd give it up, and we could get something we both liked. Hell, whether I liked it or not, I'd have consented to live in a drainpipe if that was what Cash Mitchell wanted.

Cash put his large hand on my shoulder and pushed. "My turn." His cock was hard and dripping, so I took it to mean he was more than interested in my suggestion. To sweeten the deal, I gave him my best cock-sucking skills. When he released in my mouth, I was pretty sure I had my answer, and I was happy as a clam.

We cleaned up in the sink, and I opened the door to the bathroom to find the laundry room door was open again. I walked over and closed it, not remembering if I'd closed it earlier. When it popped open again, I laughed.

"Fucking door scared the shit out of me. I thought we closed it, but apparently it doesn't stay that way. Anyway, you don't have to answer me now about the move, but say you'll think about it?" I was begging again, but god, he was worth any amount of groveling required.

"I don't need to think. We'll work it out, babe. Let's finish this up. I'm fucking tired. So, what did you think about Gregson?" Cash asked with a cute smirk.

One word came to mind. "Douche."

CHAPTER NINE

CASH

I got off the plane in Memphis and went to baggage claim to get my suitcase. I'd seen a message from my agent on my phone before we left Arizona, but there wasn't time to call him back. He probably just wanted to know how camp had gone. He was a great guy that way—no wonder Uncle Skip set me up with him.

I glanced behind me to see Cary following behind at a lazier pace, so I slowed down for him to catch up to me. We hadn't been able to sit together on the flight because there weren't two seats next to each other. I prayed to hell he hadn't changed his mind about us moving in together.

God, I needed to tell him I loved him, but I was scared to death that he'd decided it wasn't worth the shit we were going to have to go through to keep things undercover for a while. If that happened, I had no idea what I'd do.

All of the pitchers and catchers had gone out for dinner after we finished up training camp, and Cary had suggested on the bus ride to the restaurant that we should fly home that night instead of the next morning. I was grateful for the idea, because if I had to listen to fucking Gregson one more minute, I'd smother the fucker in his sleep. Plus, there was the idea of getting to sleep with Cary, so I wasn't about to disagree with the brilliant man. Cary changed our tickets, and we were off to the airport as soon as we packed our shit.

When Cary caught up with me in the terminal, I could see he was upset. "What's wrong, Brewer?"

"Nothing, really. I'm just in a bad mood. I've got shit on my mind. I'll talk to you later, Mitchell." Cary took off without another word, and he didn't stop at the carousel to get his luggage, heading directly out the front door without looking back. I immediately knew something was up.

I grabbed both of our bags and headed toward the taxi line. When I came out of the sliding doors, there were scads of photographers surrounding the place, and they had Cary trapped on the sidewalk.

"What's your response to the audio released tonight?"

"Who were you involved with in Mesa?"

"Are you gay?"

"Has the front office contacted you yet about how to handle the leak?"

"Rumor has it you're retiring to make room for a new catcher. Is that true?"

I froze. It was cold as fuck in Memphis, and I had a scarf around my neck and a beanie on my head, but Cary had blustered out of the airport wearing only a hooded Blues sweatshirt and a team cap. It was like he was fucking begging for the publicity, and I couldn't believe it.

Just then, a large man barreled through those surrounding Cary and took his hand, putting it on his shoulder. He said something to Cary that I couldn't hear, and then the two of them were off through the crowd, leaving me behind. I didn't know who the big guy was, but something was definitely off.

I felt a tap on my shoulder and turned to see my agent, Luke Schoenfeld. He was wearing a plain baseball cap and sunglasses. "Come on, Cash. We might have a problem." If Luke was there, it was worse than I could imagine. I should have called him before I left Arizona, but I was too excited about the new developments with Cary.

My contract with the Blues was for two more years, which was the max that Luke would let me sign for at the time. He'd decided I would come into my own within three seasons, and it was better to hold out for the big money until I'd proven myself. My dream had been to sign with the LA Stars, but all of that was before Cary Brewer came into my life. Now? I'd play wherever Cary played.

Luke took one of the suitcases and pulled it behind him to a large SUV waiting at the curb. "Cash, have you looked at social media? There's a story out that may or may not affect you."

I laughed. "Luke, man, I just got off a damn plane from Arizona, and my phone died right after we took off. I slept the whole way home. What's up?" We climbed into a black Suburban and were whisked away quickly.

"Mr. Schoenfeld, we have a tail. Where should we go?" Luke looked at me, and I laughed.

"My place. What's going on?" I rattled off the address to the driver, who nodded.

"Let's wait to talk until we get there." Luke glanced at the driver and then back at his phone.

Thirty minutes later, the driver pulled to the rear of my building, and we hurried out of the vehicle, leaving the luggage to be brought up. I punched in the code to open the garage door, and then Luke and I went to the service elevator inside. After we got on, I inserted my key and pressed the button for my floor. The door closed, and I turned to Luke. "What the fuck is going on?"

"There's a story that's breaking on the internet, and it's gonna be bad for Cary. I don't want you caught in the blowback."

The doors opened, and I headed off the elevator and to my door, worried to fuck. "What's this story about?"

Luke quickly punched up something on his phone and handed it to me. It was from a known gossip website, GSPOT.

SAY IT ISN'T SO! CARY BREWER, THE SEXIEST MAN IN BASEBALL, IS RETIRING!

Cary Brewer, award-winning catcher for MLB's Memphis Blues, is set to announce his retirement in the wake of a possible scandal involving an alleged affair Brewer was having with an unknown male while at Blues minicamp in Mesa, Arizona. GSPOT was given exclusive access to an audio clip that's supposed to be of Brewer and an unknown male engaging in a sexual encounter in a discreet location at the team hotel. Could it be Cary, one of the most eligible bachelors in MLB, has found true love and is ready to go off into the sunset—with a stallion instead of a mare?

My stomach sunk to the floor, and I couldn't read any more than the first paragraph. The door to the laundry room had been open when we left the bathroom. Had someone heard us? There was a link to the audio, and I wanted to fucking die. "Let me hear it. I need to know how bad it is for us." I pointed to the link. Luke stared at me for a moment, and I nodded, so he pressed the button.

"Mmm... Give it to me!"

Oh, yeah, it was the two of us, me sucking Cary off in the bathroom, though my voice was muffled by his cock in my mouth. One could definitely hear me choking a little as I was swallowing his essence.

After the gagging sound stopped, Cary could be heard clearly. *"God, that felt so good, baby. Stay here. I'll go move the kid's laundry and put ours in. I'll be back."*

Those beautiful words echoed through my mind. The two of us in the unisex john of the laundry room at the hotel taking a few minutes for ourselves. How fucking dare someone exploit our private moment! I damn well needed to talk to Cary immediately.

I pulled out my phone and started to dial his number before I remembered it was dead, but when Luke jerked it out of my hands, I was startled. "No. You can't call him. Is that you on that audio?"

I looked at Luke and saw he'd already figured it out. "Yeah. We're going to move in together. I love him," I confessed, hating that it was to my agent instead of Cary.

"*No! No!* You can't do this to me, Cash. You just finished your rookie year with great stats, and any connection to Cary Brewer could completely obliterate your career. You have to stay away from him, and don't call him. You have a week here at home. I'm going to get in touch with Dutch and Sandy, and I've already put in a call to Cary's agent, Josh Cable.

"I'm sure every player's agent has called Cable. We'll see where we are..." Luke got distracted by the ringing of his phone before he looked at the screen.

He held up his finger and answered. "Cable, what's going on?"

My heart was pounding, so while Luke was otherwise occupied, I grabbed my cell and rushed to my bedroom to plug it into a charger and call Cary's cell. After four rings, it finally answered with a shrill sound.

"We're sorry, but the number you have reached is no longer in service. Please check the number and try again. We're sorry, but the number you have reached is no longer in service. Please check the number and try again."

I hung up and tried again as the annoying voice suggested, punching in the actual digits in case the speed dial was fucked-up. I heard the same message three more times before I threw my phone against the bedroom wall. It shattered, and when Luke came running down the hall, he was definitely worried.

"You sure? Hang on."

Luke handed me the phone. "Hello?"

"Don't call me. Don't talk about me. Don't answer any questions pertaining to me. It's done." With that, the phone went dead, and my heart shattered. It was Cary, and he was done with me?

I sure as fuck didn't appreciate the banging on my door on Monday morning. I'd played hell getting Luke to leave on Saturday evening after my world went to shit, and I'd stayed in bed all day on Sunday. My phone was broken, and I didn't have a landline, so it had been nice and quiet, allowing me to cry and nap and pace the floors in peace.

I did appreciate the fact Luke was hesitant to leave me alone under the circumstances. He didn't really know me, personally, but Uncle Skip had been friends with him, and when I'd gotten called up from Nashville, Skip insisted Luke come down to Memphis from New York to cross the t's and dot the i's on my contract before I signed.

In truth, Uncle Skip had really been the driver behind the

negotiations with the Blues, making sure I was covered in every possible scenario, including the lack of a morals' clause. Once that was hammered out with the team, Skip had left me with Luke, telling me I was in good hands. At the time, I had no idea if I was or not, but based on Luke's behavior at the airport, Uncle Skip had seen to it that I wasn't vulnerable in the event he wasn't around. But, then again, I'd thought I would be in good hands with Cary and look how that shit turned out!

You weren't naïve to trust him. He loves you, and you love him. He's wigging out about that stupid fucking news story and the audio clip, justifiably so, and you're leaving him to stew on it without reminding him the two of you belong together! What the fuck are you doing?

The banging didn't stop, so I got out of bed and walked down the hall in a pair of Cary's shorts that ended up in my laundry bag, never more thankful for anything in my life than I was to have some of his clothes with me.

I opened the door to see Kim and a tall brunette woman I recognized after a fleeting moment, but this time the dress was long. There were no red nails and no makeup, but when the door closed, I was enveloped in strong arms. I couldn't help myself. I started to cry again, surprised I had any tears left to shed.

"Shh! Baby, I'm so sorry for what I said, but I'm not going to drag you under the bus with me. I love you, Cash. I'll never hurt you!" It was my Cary, and he'd told me he loved me. He pushed the wig off his head and kissed my face. I couldn't help the sobbing, so I just soaked in the feeling of being near him.

I finally got myself together and wiped my eyes on the Blues T-shirt I was wearing, which happened to be Cary's as well, pulling him with me to the living room. Kim followed behind us, appearing to be worried about us. I wanted to hug him for his concern, but I had more important fish to fry.

"What happened?" I directed my comment to Cary.

"I think an old acquaintance got pissed when I refused to help him with a pet project. He's a real prick, and I didn't like him, anyway. We played ball together in college before he dropped out and took his life in another direction. I owed him nothing, and for him to try to force me into a situation I didn't want any part of was a foolish mistake on his behalf."

I was a bit surprised by Cary's explanation, but I needed more answers. "Who the hell is it, and what the fuck was he trying to get you to do?"

"I refuse to allow him to hurt you. Let's let it go, Cash."

Hurt me? What the hell was he talking about? We were making plans—plans I hoped would go beyond either of our careers in baseball. Yes, Cary was older and likely ready to get out of the game in a few years. I was just starting out, but I had all of the confidence in the world that we could figure out a life together.

"How was he going to hurt me, Cary?"

I saw Cary Brewer's anger transform his face in a way I didn't see very often. I'd seen it a few times during the season when some asshole was trying to get over on Cary by crowding the plate. That was my catcher's territory, and as a pitcher for the Blues, I had confidence he'd protect it. Now, seeing that face in front of me let me know he'd protect me as well. "What was—who was after you, and what was he trying to force you to do?"

Cary sighed—heavily. "His name is Jeff Quattlebaum, and we were teammates at Michigan. He wanted me to work with his new pitcher—Nick Gregson—and recommend him over you to the front office.

"Jeff thought he and I had some sort of bond from college, but we damn well didn't. When I refused to support his pitcher, well, it seems like they resorted to more devious ways of undermining us." The growl in his voice as he explained things to me was sexy as hell.

I wanted to take him to bed because he was so passionate about what had happened, though I did wonder if his anger was a bit too much. "Okay, undermining seems a little over-the-top. Was there any way you could have misunderstood what he wanted you to do?"

"When I went to the bathroom before we boarded the plane back to Memphis, I got a call from Quattlebaum," Cary admitted with an angry shake of his head before he continued. "He asked me to talk to Dutch about giving Gregson another shot since he completely fucked up his tryout on Wednesday. He said if I told Dutch the kid was just nervous and he was a better pitcher than you, he'd listen.

"Quattlebaum threatened that he had something that could ruin your career, but I know the prick's just a blowhard, so I told him to fuck off. He never even fucking hinted at what he had, and hell, I couldn't imagine he'd have anything to cause a scandal, so I hung up on him.

"I might have called him a motherfucking asshole and threatened to kick his ass if he didn't leave me alone, so to retaliate, he somehow got ahold of a tape of us in that bathroom, and he leaked it. I have no idea where he got it. He had to have had us followed is all I could come up with, which is why I reacted the way I did.

"I used Josh's phone to call Luke on Saturday because Gillian had mine disconnected after the fucker wouldn't quit ringing. Stupid goddamn Quattlebaum gave out my fucking private number, too," Cary finished his explanation.

I was stunned. Why would someone go to so much trouble? The kid was good enough to get to pitch in the Triple-A League for a year or two and then get called up. Why the fuck... None of it made any sense.

"How in the fuck…" Cary seemed as stunned as me, but then I remembered a crucial piece of information that surfaced in my mind earlier.

I gasped. The goddamn laundry room door! It was open when we came out, remember? Someone must have rigged it not to lock so they could get in. How the hell did they find out we'd both be in the…"

"Shit! Gregson must have followed you downstairs." Cary added a snap of his fingers for emphasis.

I thought back to that night and what I walked into when I went back to our suite. "I don't see how he could have. He was on the phone with his girlfriend when I left, and he was still on the phone when I came back, and there were a bunch of wadded tissues on the couch next to him.

"It was obvious what he'd been doing, so I just went to bed. Hell, I wasn't in the room five minutes before Coach banged on the door to check on us," I recounted.

Cary nodded. "I missed bed check, but Rico lied for me and told Dutch I was already in bed. Luckily, Coach believed him. He took the elevator down and didn't see me in the stairwell."

"*Why* did you announce your retirement?" I couldn't imagine what must have been going through his head to make such a knee-jerk decision.

Cary shook his head, his agitation apparent. "*I didn't*. Randi Counts at SportsNet got an anonymous tip that I was going to announce my retirement because I'm gay and someone caught me with my lover. The tipster sent her that recording of us in the bathroom. She didn't release it because she couldn't verify it, but one of the gossip sites got the same call and went with it.

"I went with Randi to the ESPYs once as friends a few years ago. I know for a fact that she'd never do anything to hurt my career. She left me a voicemail while we were in the air to tell me what happened. Unfortunately, it was already out there on social media before I listened to what she'd said.

"I'm just fucking grateful they didn't say they had a picture of you coming out of the bathroom behind me, though there's nothing that says they don't. I just couldn't take the chance they hadn't turned over everything, so I'm going to retire now and take myself out of the equation.

"I was going to retire at the end of last season, anyway, but Dutch convinced me to stay on to get you settled, so I agreed to give 'em one more year. You don't need me, so it's better if I leave now and take this bullshit with me." Cary was trying to convince me, but it didn't make any sense to me.

Before I could protest, he held up a finger and continued talking. "Here's what I was thinking. I'll hold a press conference and finger Jeff Quattlebaum as my companion. He'll back off pushing Gregson to get on the team, and you're out of it completely."

"*Hell no!*" I wouldn't stand for that.

"Look, this could ruin you if anyone finds out about us. The team would cut you or send you back to Nashville until they could trade you. Honey, I'm not going anywhere, but you deserve to have the career you want. Maybe in the future, we can be open about our relationship, but I don't want to fuck things up for you." His words touched me, but... *no!*

I pulled him into my arms. "I won't let you sacrifice yourself. We need to know who taped us."

"How the hell could we find out?"

I considered his question, and all my time watching cop shows instead of studying back in high school and college paid off. "Maybe the hotel could help us? They have security tapes, right?"

Kim laughed behind us. "That's brilliant! As a matter of

fact, I know a guy who can help with this. He used to work for the DEA! He comes into the club when he's in town, and he's a really great guy."

I wasn't surprised at all that Kim would know someone, but Cary appeared skeptical. "Yeah? Who?"

"He works in the personal protection business. His name is London St. Michael, and he lives in New York where he works for a company called Golden Elite Associates-America. It's home base is in Italy, I think. Anyway, he vacations down in Miami and stops in to see us at the club when he's in town. Let me call him and see if he has any ideas." Without waiting for an answer from us, Kim walked down the hallway to my bedroom and closed the door.

I turned to look at Cary, finally laughing. "I don't guess you have that sexy thong and garter thing on under that ugly dress, do you?"

He laughed and held up the hem of the too-big garment, showing me jeans and sneakers. "When I called Kim for help, he didn't waste any time. He flew up, and we went to a discount store and bought this." Cary held the flowered thing away from him as if it had cooties, which made me chuckle.

I helped him take it off, tossing it and the wig from the floor over the back of a chair, and I pulled him over to the couch so we could sit down. "If I come out with you, we can fight this thing together." Maybe I wasn't exactly ready, but with Cary, I'd weather any storm.

I could see he was going to fight me, but I wasn't having it. Yes, Cary was older, but I wasn't stupid. Together, we were a hell of a team on the field, and we could be one off the field, as well. He just needed to see it for himself and give me a chance.

CHAPTER TEN

CARY

"Baby, no. You're not coming out until, and if, you're ready to do so. I'll get Gillian to set up a press conference for tomorrow morning at Blues Stadium. I'll go out there and tender my letter of..."

"No, you won't, or I'll call Randi Counts right now and give her an exclusive about how big your dick is and how sweet your cream tastes. You think you're gonna play the fucking martyr? Bullshit. I absolutely refuse to let you do this alone, Cary!" I could see my man was just getting started, and I wanted to kiss him for how much of a fighter I was sure he could be. I damn well wanted him on my side.

"I want you to think about this overnight. You don't have to blow up your career for me to love you," I reminded him.

Kim came back into the living room. "Okay, I spoke to my friend, London. He's flying out to Mesa in the morning, and I told him you guys would by flying out toward the end of the week for training camp, so he'll be around to meet with you. Cash, I saw your broken phone on the floor of your bedroom, so I'll just run out and get you one of those pay-as-you-go jobs. I'll also stop and get us something for lunch since I'm betting you have no food. I should be gone about an hour, boys. One hour..." Kim walked out the front door, pulling it closed behind him.

I turned to look at Cash to see he was smiling. "Come on," he insisted, so I followed him down the hallway.

"Are those my shorts... and my shirt?" I barely recognized my own shit because I was distracted by his fantastic ass.

Cash let go of my hand and quickly whisked off the shirt and dropped the shorts, picking them up and handing them to me. "They were mixed in with my laundry. You probably have some of my stuff, too."

Seeing his beautiful naked body had me hard in an instant, all of my anger over Quattlebaum and his bullshit melted away. I quickly stripped and followed Cash to the unmade bed, looking around to see several empty beer bottles and empty chip bags. When I hopped into his bed, I felt crumbs under my ass and started to laugh. "What the hell did you do in this bed?"

Cash climbed in and right back out. "Son of a bitch. Get out and we can fold the top sheet up for now. Sorry about this, but I've been licking my wounds here since Saturday night." He then pulled me out of bed.

I felt a pull at my heart upon hearing his words, so instead of the two of us continuing to hurt and stew over what was the best thing to do, I looked into his gorgeous eyes. "I love you. Let me lick your wounds now." We pulled up the top sheet before we lay down again and proceeded to lick each other everywhere we could reach.

After prep and a condom, I settled him between my legs. "Seriously, you should really think twice about coming out before you make a mistake you can't take back."

Cash leaned forward and kissed my lips as he pressed inside me, the burn more than welcome. I'd missed having him inside me. It always felt right when we made love, and I never wanted it to end.

Once he was settled, Cash stopped. "While I have you here and you can't get away without maiming me which wouldn't be in either of our best interests, I have a proposal—well, actually, I want you to think about something as well. I still want to move in with you, but I want... I think it's a good idea if we get married." He immediately closed his eyes so he couldn't see my reaction.

The words caught me completely by surprise, no doubt. Without waiting for me to offer any thoughts on the matter—not that I had any—he began moving inside me and hitting my prostate perfectly, which, in turn, rendered me incapable of uttering a single word.

Wednesday morning, I was at the airport again, though way too fucking early. I'd talked to Cash about eight times the day before on our new shitty phones, and we'd decided going to the airport separately was the best idea. I'd found us flights later in the day, but when I'd sent the text to him with the details, he told me he'd already handled it and I should cancel the flights. He also told me to meet him at the airport at the asscrack of dawn—six in the morning. We were going to talk about that shit because I didn't get up that early if I didn't have to, and he should have remembered that from Miami.

I saw him in line at Cinnabon, which made me laugh. He hated the damn things, so why the hell was he in line? I walked over to where he was standing. "You can't take that through security, remember? Isn't there a place on the other side of security if you want coffee?"

Cash laughed. "Grab our bags and follow me."

I laughed and pulled up the handle on his roller bag, dragging both bags behind me toward the check-in desk. My guess was we'd check our bags, eat—or I would—and then we'd head through security. When Cash continued past the automated machines for self-check, I became confused. "Mitchell, where…"

"Come on. We're gonna be late, and we have a flight plan that won't wait." Cash was carrying two cups of coffee and a Cinnabon bag, and he headed toward a TSA agent waiting by a restricted exit.

"Mr. Mitchell?"

Cash nodded, and the agent opened the door for us. I followed my man through the entrance, nodding at the agent as we walked down a long hallway and into a lobby I never knew existed.

"Where the hell are we going?" I asked as I looked around to see nice leather chairs and glass-topped tables instead of the shitty rows of seats available in the main terminal to wait for flights.

The elegantly appointed area was small, maybe seating for twenty people, but there were televisions everywhere, and pleasant-looking men and women walked the area with happy smiles to check on those waiting.

We stood near the entrance, and a woman wearing a smart pantsuit with an odd insignia over a nameplate on the left breast pocket of her navy jacket approached us. "Mr. Mitchell? Welcome, sir. I'm Bridget, your flight liaison. I received a call that your flight crew is ready to go. Allow me to have a skycap take your bags to X-ray so they can be loaded on your flight. Once we get the okay, I'll escort you out to your jet, and you'll be on the way to your destination shortly."

She then turned to smile at me. "Welcome, Mr. Brewer."

Bridget then lifted her hand and motioned two fingers to a gentleman standing behind a counter.

The guy was dressed in a pair of navy trousers with a matching vest over a crisp white dress shirt. He took the bags from me and wheeled them over to a large X-ray machine as Bridget checked our identification, pecking information into a tablet she was holding. After the young man returned with our bags, the two of them escorted us out to a waiting plane—a jet of some sort that I couldn't identify. I'd flown on private jets before, of course, because the team had a plane, but never had I flown in one like the fancy one waiting for us.

I turned to look at Cash. "Really? A private plane? We could have flown commercial, kid." I bumped shoulders with him as we walked out onto the tarmac and up the staircase adjacent to the private jet.

"We could have, but I wanted my boyfriend to travel in style," Cash replied with a wink.

"Boyfriend, huh?" I shook my head at how excited he seemed to be as we ascended the stairs.

"Oh, uh, for now," Cash responded as he went through the door ahead of me.

"Welcome aboard. I'm Mika, and I'll be your flight attendant today. Can I take your coats?" the young woman with short, brown hair greeted us as she held out her arm.

We both took off our coats and handed them to the lady before I took in the sight before me. The plane was gorgeous. The furnishings were shades of beige and tan, and it was pretty damn classy.

The flight attendant motioned us forward. I glanced around to see polished mahogany finished with gold lamps on glass end tables. The flight attendant came out with two crystal flutes filled with champagne or sparkling wine, and she winked at Cash, which surprised me.

He took both of the glasses from her and grinned. "Thank you, Mika. We're ready to go when the crew is ready." Cash directed me to a pair of chairs that were like recliners with seat belts so we could finish our champagne. The young woman collected the glasses and left us alone.

Mika stopped at the open cockpit door to speak to the pilot and co-pilot, and then she closed it before buckling into a jump seat. Next thing I knew, we were flying down the runway in a private jet on our way to spring training. I was guessing my day could have been worse.

I hadn't really slept well the night before, wishing Cash was next to me, so when I had his hand in mine, I was out. I felt a blanket being placed over me before Cash gently pulled his hand from mine and tucked me in. I missed his warmth immediately, but knowing he was near was a huge comfort.

"Thanks, Mika. I'll wake him up in a minute. I think it should only take us a few hours, and then we'll be back."

Mika whispered in return. "The reservation I received from the scheduler a few moments ago confirmed the noon slot. The message I received was that you should arrive thirty minutes prior to your reservation. It takes about fifteen minutes to get there. We'll be here waiting. May I offer my congratulations?"

"Not yet. I'm not sure if he'll go for it, so let's not jinx me."

It was the strangest dream I'd ever had in my life!

I was jarred awake and suddenly thrust forward in my seat, which was fucking horrifying from a sound sleep. The plane was listing left and right, and when I opened my eyes and turned toward Cash, he was white-knuckling the arms of his seat. "Christ! What's happening? Where are we?"

"I was beginning to wonder if you were dead." Cash took my hand and held on to it as the plane finally touched down and then began to taxi down the runway. I glanced out the window next to me, seeing mountains. Where the fuck were we?

"I didn't sleep well last night without you next to me. Where the hell are we?" I asked as I sat forward and stretched a bit.

The plane stopped in front of a small airport I'd never seen before. The sign, "Henderson Executive Airport," was on the side of a large brick building with palm trees and cacti dotting the desert landscape. The jet stopped several yards from the building, and the door was opened, stairs folding down to the ground.

I saw a black limo slowly drive toward us and stop. Mika, the flight attendant, stepped forward with two steaming towels. "If you'd like to freshen up, you're welcome to use the lav before you go. We'll be here when you're finished, and I'll have a nice snack for you when you return. Enjoy your day." The woman's mysterious smile had me worried.

Cash nodded, taking my hand and leading me down the stairs. Once we were on the tarmac, the car pulled closer. A woman dressed in a black suit with neat, dark hair pulled back in a bun and wearing a pair of aviator sunglasses stepped out and walked to the back of the limo, opening the door. "Gentlemen, welcome to Las Vegas."

Cash basically pushed me inside before he followed, closing the door. There was a bottle of expensive champagne in a bucket and two glasses shoved into the ice to chill, and I was so fucking confused, I couldn't begin to comprehend what the fuck was happening. "Why are we in Vegas?"

The door slammed, and the woman walked around the car and hopped into the front, rolling up the tinted window between the front and back compartments.

Cash picked up the bottle and poured each of us a glass of bubbly. "There are times when action is required, and this is one of those times. I'm sorry I didn't give you a heads-up, but I knew with a man like you, the element of surprise was my best tool. You love me?" I glanced up, seeing he was dead serious.

"Yeah... Yes, I love you. I don't lie, Cash." I hoped he wasn't going to try to change my mind about retiring so he could stay undercover. I did love him, and I didn't want him to question if I was doing the right thing. Hell, I didn't want to question it, either.

"Okay. So, should we get lunch and maybe gamble a little? We deserve some time to ourselves, and seriously, we can get lost in Vegas and nobody will know or give a fuck who we are." Cash reached for a bag in the back seat across from where we sat and opened it, pulling out two New York Liberty baseball caps. He handed one to me, and we both laughed as the car drove out of the airport property, headed for the Strip.

It was a cool morning—fifties or low sixties if I had to guess, and the sun was shining. It was still a lot warmer than it had been in Memphis when we left earlier that morning. I was happy to feel the sunshine on my face.

We left the airport and headed toward the I-15, then taking the 215, and finally, exiting to Las Vegas Boulevard. We drank the champagne, and when the car pulled into the long driveway for Caesar's Palace, I was totally ready to have a great fucking time because starting the next day, we'd be in training camp, and there would be no fun until the season started in April.

We walked into the casino through the marbled entrance, seeing all of the statues and grandeur one would expect to see. I'd been to Vegas a couple of times over the years, but based on the awed expression on Cash's face, I could tell my young boyfriend hadn't.

"Would you like a drink?" His voice seemed a bit shaky, and I wondered why.

I chuckled at his nerves. "Do you not have your ID? I'll get 'em."

Cash didn't answer, instead looking away and asking, "What to drink?"

I wondered what the hell had suddenly replaced his happy attitude with nerves, but hopefully, if I got a little liquor in him, he'd show his hand. "Hell, I'll have a Crown on the rocks."

Cash hurried over to the bar and ordered for us, paying the bartender and leaving a generous tip. He handed me my glass and we walked over to a roulette table.

"You gamble?" Cash asked.

"Yeah, a little. Some of us guys on the team used to get together every month for cards in the off-season, but it sorta fell apart because they had families who needed their time and attention. I miss it, sometimes. It was great to get to know people better off the field. It helped with team building. We were all much more comfortable to keep in touch over the winter break, just talking about anything other than baseball." I remembered how we used to talk more about bullshit than we played cards. I'd had a good time with them, and decided to suggest we take up the practice again.

"Huh. I learned how to play roulette when I was at Florida State. One of the guys had a mini wheel, and on Sunday nights after everybody was back from seeing family over the weekends, we'd all venture to the basement of the library and gamble. I made enough playing cards and roulette to subsidize some of the fees I was being charged so I didn't have to get loans. So, pick your game. My treat." Cash's sullen nerves had turned into an unusual giddiness, which was a bit strange.

The two of us stepped up to a table to buy chips. Cash gave me a quick primer on the basics of the game, and we bet, me taking the safe bets of odd or even and red or black. It was fun to just hang out like any other guys having a little fun in Vegas, both of us with sunglasses and caps in place, not that anyone gave a shit. We definitely didn't draw attention from the gambling crowd because professional gamblers wore sunglasses all the time.

The other great thing about gambling in Vegas was that you could drink for free. After a couple of drinks, I noticed Cash was getting a little braver with his wagers. When he put a grand on thirteen black, I held my fucking breath.

I'd come from white-trash parents who'd blown up our home while cooking drugs, taking out my little brother in the process. Hell, that thousand dollars Cash was planning to bet could have been the difference between life and death in my family, but those days were gone.

I touched Cash's hand. "Dude, seriously? I'm sure you have a good contract, but that's a lot of money."

Cash downed his drink and turned to me, leaning forward and kissing my lips. "I tell you what. If I win this one, then you don't retire. We live our lives as a couple, and you'll agree with whatever idiotic scheme I come up with to deal with that bullshit tape. I'll donate my winnings to the charity of your choice, and we'll live happily ever after.

"If I lose, then I'll double the donation to a charity of your choice, and I'll wait a while to come out. I won't bitch at you about your ill-conceived plan to retire and claim that asshole is your boyfriend, and we'll stay undercover for a few more years. Deal?" He held out his hand, and I considered his proposition.

I didn't really want to stay on the down-low with Cash, but I also didn't like the alternative of him being railroaded out of baseball because of who he loved—me. I wasn't letting him go, and I didn't want him to let me go, either.

I wasn't a mathematician who could figure the odds of him winning that bet or of us making it long term. I had a half-assed degree in marketing, but I'd never believed I'd use it, and hell, I only made grades good enough to keep my scholarship to play baseball. Deciding which way to go was going to have to be a gut decision, but I knew beyond the shadow of a doubt that he was my future.

"Okay, thirteen black. You're on."

Cash pulled his hands back from the chips to release them to the dealer, before he wrapped an arm around my waist, pulling me in front of him as we watched that little white ball circle counterclockwise.

Cash moved closer and placed his hand on my stomach as he wrapped around me. When I glanced over my shoulder, I noticed he'd turned his cap backward, and his handsome chin was resting on my shoulder. He'd also moved his sunglasses behind his neck.

"Are you having fun?" I asked, not pushing him away or moving out of his embrace, no matter how many disgusted looks we got from the other players.

"I'm having a ball, as a matter of fact. So, when I win, you're going to let me have my way?"

I couldn't help but laugh at him. "Sure. When you win $35,000 dollars, you can have your way, Cash."

I could feel Cash's head turning like mine as we watched the ball. "Why is this so important to you?" I just had to ask because his behavior was so different than usual. One of the things I loved about him was when he was shy and not cocksure like when he was on the pitcher's mound. He owned that fucking mound, and he knew it, but off that spot of dirt in the middle of the field, Cash Mitchell was a different guy—shy, hesitant, eager to please.

As I watched him, I could see he wasn't sure about something, but he was fighting his instincts to shy away from whatever he had planned. He wanted something awfully bad, but I just didn't know what.

Cash took a deep breath and exhaled. The sweet scent of Jack and ginger on his breath caught my attention and sent a little chill down my spine. "If I win, then you have to do what I say, and I say we get married and go to training camp as a couple. Let's see what they do about that?"

"Thank you. No more bets, please..." The little white ball skipped from pocket to pocket before settling. "And the winner is thirteen. Thirteen black!"

CHAPTER ELEVEN

CARY

"Do you, Cash Allen Mitchell, take Cary Dean Brewer to be your lawfully wedded husband..."

"I do."

"Do you, Cary Dean Brewer, take Cash Allen Mitchell to be your lawfully wedded husband? To have and to hold for the rest of your life? For better or worse? Through richer or poorer, sickness and health, forsaking all others to keep yourself only for him until death parts you?"

"I definitely do."

"Then, by the power vested in me by Clark County in the great State of Nevada, I now pronounce you married. You may kiss your husband."

We kissed, and then Billy Idol's voice came through the speakers singing "White Wedding."

I couldn't hold the laugh. "You picked that?"

"No, but they play it for everyone... Little White Wedding Chapel? Get it? It kinda fits, I guess. So, uh, thanks for marrying me," Cash announced like he was thanking me for bringing in the trash cans from the curb. Of course, I cracked up when he extended his fist for me to bump. The shyness coming out of him when he didn't know what to say had me grinning from ear to ear.

Cash laughed with me and took my hand, leading me out of the Little White Wedding Chapel. The car was waiting for us, and ten minutes later, we were being shuffled into a steakhouse that didn't open until five o'clock in the evening according to the sign on the door.

It was called the Golden Calf, and it definitely looked like a place where Frank, Dean, and the boys would have spent many booze-and-cigarette-filled nights. Dark wood-paneled walls gave it a classic Vegas feel, and the mannequins dressed like Vegas royalty—Elvis, Wayne Newton, Liberace—were seated at a table in the corner like they were having dinner together after a show.

Garnet-colored glass and brass lamps hung over each table, and small, discreet spotlights were focused on brass plaques affixed to the walls by each table, a celebrity's name engraved into them for posterity alongside their framed, autographed picture from a time when they'd eaten at the restaurant when each celebrity had been a hot commodity.

The room was filled with red leather, half-moon booths that lined the walls of the whole room, and small two- and four-top tables with red leather chairs filled in the space in the center. We were guided to a booth in the back corner of the dining room by a man in a tuxedo who wore a welcoming smile.

The booth had been set up with an elegant white tablecloth and a candle, a polished silver bucket holding a bottle of expensive champagne was on the left side, and two sparkling crystal glasses were sitting on the table in the middle. The restaurant didn't have any windows in the dining room, so it was hard to tell if it was day or night, but the whole scene was very romantic.

Cash extended his hand, so I got in and stopped in the middle of the seat. He slid in on the other side and sat close to me, placing his arm around the back of the booth as he looked up at the man who was patiently waiting for us to get settled so he could give us the two leather portfolios in his hand.

Cash leaned forward and kissed my cheek. "Cool place, yeah? The lady at the wedding chapel helped me set it up when I called about the ceremony. She said she and her husband eat here for every wedding anniversary, so I figured it must be good. They've been married for forty years, she told me. It seems like a pretty good way to begin a tradition for the rest of our lives, huh?" His eagerness for my approval made my heart skip a beat.

"... *the rest of our lives, huh?*" Suddenly the weight of those words landed on me as I looked into his beautiful, whiskey-brown eyes. We were married, for better or worse, as the man had said during the vows.

I'd finally gotten married, which would have surprised everyone I used to know. Hell, it would surprise everyone I knew now, and the enormity of what we had done and what would happen to both of us was like a bucket of ice water.

The waiter placed the black leather folders in front of us and smiled. "Welcome to the Golden Calf. I'm Romeo, and I'll be taking care of you today. May I pour?" He motioned toward the bottle in the silver bucket.

"I need to use the facilities. Uh, where's the men's room?" I asked, hoping to hold down the drinks I'd already consumed that morning.

The man nodded and directed me to the back of the bar where the restrooms were located. I went inside and locked the door, taking a deep breath as I braced my hands on the sink and looked into the mirror. "What the fuck did you just do?"

I could hear Dean Martin singing over the speakers, "How

lucky could one man be?" That was when all of the stars seemed to align in my mind—I seriously was the luckiest son of a bitch in the world, and I was in the bathroom, trying not to puke? What the fuck was wrong with me?

I looked at the ten-dollar silver band on my finger that Cash had bought from the couple at the wedding chapel, and I laughed.

"Fuck! I completely forgot to get us rings to exchange. I'm so..." He then turned to the officiant. "It's still legal, right? I mean if we don't have rings, that doesn't mean it's not legal, does it?" He looked so cute with the worried look on his face that I wanted to haul his ass out of there to a dark corner somewhere.

Of course, the fucking guy opened the podium where he was standing behind and pulled out a blue velvet tray with silver and gold rings in various sizes. They damn well weren't real.

I dared not laugh, but it was comical. "I'm a size eleven."

"Ten," Cash added. The man picked two of the silver ones and smiled, offering the Cash's ring to me and mine to him.

"That'll be twenty dollars." I started to reach for my wallet when Cash whipped out a twenty from his and handed it to the man.

"Wow, I'm getting off cheap." I could see he was embarrassed he hadn't remembered the rings. I wanted to kiss him right there.

I smiled at the memory before I grabbed my phone from my pocket and called Gillian. "Hey, Cary! Good to hear from you. I'll be coming out to Mesa next week. Are you excited for the beginning of training camp? I want to get some action shots with the team to use for some of the endorsement deals I'm working on."

"Yeah, uh, thrilled. Look, you're going to need to issue a press release within the next few days. Can you come out sooner? Also, will you make me a reservation and..."

If Cash and I were going to do something that could signal the end of our careers, we were going to go into the breach with guns blazing.

"There's something wrong with the plane. Mika just called me. We can't take off until tomorrow morning," Cash told me after we finished eating the best fucking steak I'd ever had in my life. The food was delicious, and Romeo was an amazing waiter. He was attentive, but he didn't crowd us. It was really nice.

"Well, we could fly commercial and get there tonight, or we can wait for them to fix the plane and then fly out in the morning. What do you think?" We were due in Mesa the next day, and a team meeting had been scheduled for three o'clock after everyone arrived. We could be there by then for sure.

It was our wedding night, and fucking all night sounded like the best idea in the world, which was why I had Gillian make the call to arrange it. I owed the woman a lot for being so fucking organized, but I figured her six-figure salary probably more than covered it.

Cash turned to me, worry etching his features. "What would we do tonight?"

"Well, it's our wedding night, and I got us a suite at the Venetian, so you tell me what you think we should do," I couldn't help taunting, seeing the surprise I was hoping I'd get.

Cash's face turned red. "I was afraid you were trying to climb out the window in the bathroom to run back to the chapel to get Mr. Columbus to undo it."

I wasn't about to tell him how close to right he was, but seeing him sitting there with a cheap-ass band like the one on my finger made me think about the beautiful life we could have together, and it stopped me in my tracks.

"Never. I called Gillian to come to Mesa on Friday. You don't have a publicist, so you should call Luke to come out as well, and I'll call Josh. We need the whole team on this one because the news is going to hit hard. Meanwhile, we need time for us, and I made a few plans of my own."

My handsome groom nodded and glanced to the server, who snapped his fingers. A young guy came out with a piece of cheesecake with cherry sauce and a candle in it. I looked at Cash, seeing a big-ass grin on his face, and I knew everything was going to be fucking fine.

"You're walking a little funny there, Pitcher," I teased as I followed Cash through the private terminal after we landed at the Mesa airport. The night before had been so incredible I wished to fuck I had taped it.

"Lunch was amazing, babe," I mentioned as we stood in the huge white-marble shower of our honeymoon suite. Gillian had pitched a fit when I'd told her what I'd done by eloping, but she'd booked the best room in the place for me—reminding me three times that she wasn't a personal assistant.

Champagne and chocolate-covered strawberries I hadn't asked for were waiting on the coffee table in the living room of the suite, and there was soft music playing in the background when we opened the door. A trail of red had been scattered on the floor leading to the bedroom, and there on the bed was the heart-shaped outline of red rose petals. It was like something out of an old rom-com, but the look on Cash's face had me grinning with satisfaction at surprising him as he'd surprised me.

"It really was good. I need to let it digest a little before we consummate this bitch. How about we walk over to the mall and get some stuff? We're going to need to have clean underwear for tomorrow. Our bags are still with the plane," Cash reminded me. I wanted to laugh at his assessment, but he was dead-on.

I nodded. "I should have told Gillian to have Mika send them to us when I asked her to set this up." The room was fucking amazing, but the awe on Cash's face made Gillian's complaints worth every second.

I glanced around, taking in the decor. The furniture and drapery were teal and grey, and the bedroom was white with touches of both. The bathroom was huge, and it was all luxurious. I'd stayed in nice places, but nothing like the Presidential Suite at the Venetian Hotel and Casino.

When Cash didn't respond, I turned to see him standing behind the teal sofa, a sheepish look on his face. "What did you do?"

Cash swallowed. "I called them, too, while you were in the bathroom at the restaurant and asked them to hold off on the flight until tomorrow. I didn't know you'd called someone to do the same thing.

"I wanted us to stay in town tonight, and I was planning to find us a place to stay, but you took care of it. I put the crew in a nice casino hotel in Henderson. They weren't complaining about the change of plans.

"I just wanted us to have tonight, Cary, but clearly, you did, too. I mean, we just got married. I know neither of us is mushy, but I thought... Well, I wanted us to have one night to ourselves. I know when we get to Mesa and we tell Dutch we got married, the shit will hit the fan, and it's not gonna be pretty. Let's take this one day and night for us." It was exactly what I'd concluded when I was in the bathroom at the Golden Calf. We were more in sync than I'd actually considered.

After we each took a turn in the john, we went downstairs and through the casino, exiting the building. We walked down the sidewalk along the driveway and made a left when we got to Las Vegas Boulevard, heading the mile up the street to the mall.

We bought necessities, ball caps and sunglasses in place, and then we stopped at the Paris Hotel and Casino to have a beer at their rooftop beer garden. We sat at a two-top table near the bar. Again, we were fortunate that nobody recognized us.

We had a few beers and people watched for a while before we went to the CVS next door for more necessities—things more important than underwear and socks.

The cashier at CVS gave us a strange look when we placed our basket on the counter, but she didn't say anything about the fact we had four enema kits. After we paid, we walked back to the hotel and set about our tasks, thankful for two bathrooms. An hour and private showers later, we popped that champagne and got busy.

"Wanna sixty-nine while we get each other ready? You can go first because I've got that recovery time thing. I'll hold off, and after you fuck me—if I can keep from coming—I'll rock your world, Pitcher!"

Cash's face lit up at my comment. "Sounds like a plan, Catcher!" I was sure mine did as well.

I swirled my tongue around Cash's beautiful cock as I lay on the bed while Cash was on all fours hovering over me and giving me his best. His tongue was a tool for sin, and my young husband didn't really have a gag reflex unless I was cramming my cock down his throat as I had when that fucking tape was made. It would take my best to keep up with him.

Cash pulled off my cock. "God, if we keep going, I'll blow, and that's not what I want to do. Can we, uh... can we get to the main event?"

"Sure. How do you want me?"

"Just like this," Cash commanded, climbing off me and

turning around, picking up the lube we'd been using to get each other ready and slicking up his cock.

Cash settled between my spread legs after he pushed a pillow under my ass. "I'll go as slow as I can, babe. I don't want to hurt you, but god, I'm so fucking torqued about us getting married, I'm not sure if I can control myself. Tell me to stop if I'm too rough." Cash hovered over me, kissing my neck as he slowly brushed his cock over my hole before slowly pressing it inside.

I gasped when he bit my neck as he pushed against my prostate. "Damn, you learned pretty fucking well how to do that!" I tried to think about anything other than the intoxicating feeling of the blunt mushroom head gliding over my sweet spot as he continued to slide into me.

I wasn't all that fucking intellectual, but it was everything I believed a wedding night should be. I was pretty certain I'd only have one—because I had no intentions of ever doing it again. Being married to Cash Mitchell was all I ever needed.

Cash lifted my legs up to his broad shoulders and continued thrusting, but not pounding, always mindful of the physicality of things so I wouldn't have problems with my catcher's stance when we began practicing at camp. Oh, god, it felt so fucking good. I tried like hell to hold off, but I couldn't stop from erupting between us as he continued his robust rhythm.

We'd had physicals and testing when we were in Mesa for pitchers' and catchers' week, and we'd both received results that we tested negative for all STDs. We'd both had HIV testing done as well, which wasn't unusual for players because guys fucked around, and the team doctors insisted on knowing the state of our health.

We'd both tested negative so we hadn't bothered to buy condoms at the drug store. It felt incredible to have Cash leave *something of himself inside me, and when it was my turn, I made sure Cash Mitchell knew he was mine.*

"Fuck you, Catcher. Oh! There's our ride." Cash pointed to a man in a black suit with a sign that read "Mitchell & Brewer."

I caught up to him, and we walked over to the man, who already had our luggage. "We're Mitchell and Brewer. How'd you know when we were getting in?"

The young man smiled. "Ms. Windell set it up. I'm to give you a ride out to your hotel. She said I should tell you that Mr. Weingarten and Mr. James are waiting for you."

Cash shrugged and turned to me, "I guess we're going into it headfirst, huh?"

"I pay Gillian a hell of a lot of money, so she damn well better do her job. Obviously, she's started the ball rolling with the team, so let's see what happens. Come on, we can't be late to meet with Daddy and Uncle Dutch."

We both snickered at my comment before we followed the driver out of the terminal. The shit was about to hit the fan, but I had Cash next to me, and I knew we'd defend each other till death did we part—just like we'd promised in our vows.

CHAPTER TWELVE

CASH

I was worried about what was going to happen when we got to the hotel in Mesa, but as I squirmed in the back of the SUV that was taking us to training camp, I remembered every touch and every kiss from our wedding night. When I glanced at Cary, and he winked, I knew we would always defend each other, regardless of the opponent. I never had to do anything alone again. That was a fucking relief!

We arrived at the hotel and checked in before Cary was given a note. He opened it and smirked before showing it to me. It was from Dutch, the head coach of the team.

We're waiting on your country ass in the conference room on 5. You better show up the minute your feet hit the ground. Brewer, I mean it. I don't have time for bullshit.

Cary and I both chuckled as we headed to the elevator. The driver, Jack, was going to take our bags up to our room—we'd been assigned to the same room as preseason, which was a fucking relief. I did wonder, though, if that would change when they found out we were married.

We stepped onto the elevator, and Cary punched in the

button for five. I pulled him close and kissed him, smiling as I looked into his gorgeous eyes. "Think they'll reassign our rooms? They're going to shit a brick about this, you know. I didn't realize you'd asked your publicist to call a meeting."

Cary shook his head. "I seriously didn't. I did tell her we got married and asked her to do me a couple of favors. I guess she figured it was better for us to get out in front of it, which isn't a bad idea.

"The quick answer about the rooms? Probably. Look, I play every game, but you don't pitch back to back. I did, however, have a thought. I want us to work on your changeup, babe. If you can get more confident with it, there's no way they'll get between us or make a big deal about the fact we're married. We already know you're a hot commodity, so if we play it right, they can't afford to get rid of either of us.

"Now, this is the part you're not going to like. I want you to work with Rico Suarez. I want you to be able to work with any catcher, not just me. When I retire next year, I'm going to push Dutch to replace me with Suarez, not to go out to look for another catcher. I mean, come on—who could replace me? At least I can train the kid while I'm still around." Cary laughed and nudged my ribs with his elbow.

Cary then continued, this time with a serious look in his eyes. "I'm going to ask Sandy to bring the kid up so I can work with him in the bullpen until after the All-Star break. I then want you to work with him more.

"Rico is a really nice kid, and I think you'd get along well with him once you got to know him better. I know you only talked at dinner that night when that asshat Gregson was with us, but Suarez is a guy you'd probably have a lot in common with.

"I'm also going to do everything I can to see that Gregson

never dresses out in a Blues uniform." Based on the look on Cary's face, I could tell he meant it.

When we stepped off the elevator and headed toward the conference room, I took Cary's hand and stopped him. I looked at the cheap wedding ring I'd bought at the spur of the moment, and I gently slid it off his finger, doing the same with my own.

"I think for this first meeting, maybe we should keep these out of sight?" I slipped both rings into the pocket of my jeans, immediately missing the feeling of the metal, regardless of how cheap, against my skin to remind me of the new chapter we'd begun.

Cary, my strong, brave husband, leaned forward and offered a gentle kiss before we walked the few feet to the conference room, and I knocked on the door. "In!"

I turned to Cary, and he nodded, so I opened the door. I didn't expect there to be five people sitting around that table, but when I glanced at Cary, he didn't flinch.

My agent, Luke, was there, and of course, I knew Coach Weingarten and the GM, Sandy James. I'd met Cary's agent, Josh, before, but the woman wasn't anyone I'd ever seen.

"Ah, the dream team," Dutch commented, not hiding the sarcasm in his voice. The look on his face told me he'd rather beat the shit out of me than even consider I played for his team—the baseball one, not the sexual one. Based on the dissatisfied look on his face, I was guessing he knew I'd never played on his sexual team, either.

"Sit down, gentlemen," Sandy ordered. My ass hurt from the previous night, but I had a feeling it was about to be completely annihilated when they got done with us. I just wondered how they found out.

CHAPTER THIRTEEN

CARY

I glanced in Cash's direction to see how he wanted to play it, but when he pulled out my chair and extended his hand, my serious composure cracked. I sat down and pulled out his chair, patting the seat. Cash sat next to me, both of us snickering at the looks on Sandy's and Dutch's faces. Oh, it wasn't going to be pretty when they found out everything, but I decided I didn't give a flying fuck.

I determined it was now or never, so I turned to Gillian. "Were you able to pick them up for me?"

I'd contacted the jeweler and ordered the rings myself, but I didn't want them mailed to me. I had asked Gillian to pick them up for me in Los Angeles. The store was near her office, anyway.

I knew my publicist wasn't too happy about me asking her to do a personal errand, but she pulled two red boxes from her bag and slid them over the table to me. I flipped open one of the boxes, seeing a little tag that read, "size ten," so I pulled the platinum band with a beautiful gold filigree overlay from the box and turned to Cash. "I took the liberty..."

I slid the other box over to him before I took his hand. "You made all of the other plans, so I did this. If you don't like them, then we can go together to get something else. I'll order each of us a neck chain so we can still have them with us when we play. I know it's kind of silly, but it's a symbol of our commitment, and I want to be able to touch it and remember how fucking lucky I am." I didn't bother to look around the room to see the reactions from those in attendance.

"You don't like the ten-dollar rings I bought us?" Cash joked as he extended his finger with a big grin.

I slid the ring into place and held on to his hand for a moment. "Those other ones might have given us gangrene! I think these are a little better."

Cash opened the other box and held out the ring, sliding it on my finger as well. I turned my hand to look at it and grinned before doing a little chair dance of happiness for the benefit of the crowd.

I then turned to Cash, holding up my fist. My man didn't disappoint. He bumped it, and then we both turned to the table to see confusion and complete shock. At least Gillian giggled.

"So, now that *that's* out in the open, what else can we do for you?" I wasn't hiding the joy I felt at having Cash next to me.

I saw Dutch sit up and glance between the two of us before he spoke. "Gillian called me and said you wanted to see us to talk about a possible announcement, so here we are. Now, what the fuck is this ring business all about? You two going steady or something, Brewer?"

I turned to Cash and saw that shy smile, so I reached for his hand. "Well, we kinda got married in Vegas. So, how do you boys wanna proceed?"

"*You did what?*" The unison of the four voices around the table wasn't exactly like a choir of angels.

I turned to my husband. "You got anything to say?"

Cash winked before he turned to the group. "We haven't had the chance to register for gifts yet, but we'll email you when we have, though it might not be until after we take the team to the World Series."

That made me crack up—loudly. I turned to Cash. "We're going to the World Series?"

"You said you wanted to retire next year, so this is our year to do it. Are you reconsidering leaving?"

"No, babe. I have a job offer in Miami as an assistant coach, and with the settlement I think we'll get from the Blues, I have every confidence we'll be fine," I taunted.

"*What* settlement?" It was Sandy, and I wasn't surprised at all. He was the general manager, and any talk of money always made his face turn as red as his hair.

Cash turned to look at Luke Schoenfeld, his agent, who seemed as baffled as anyone else at the table. "I believe he's referring to the settlement we'll get when we file a wrongful termination or breach of contract lawsuit against the Blues because they're probably going to try to fire us for being together.

"Yes, we're married. We got married yesterday, and we have no desire to annul it or terminate it in any way. Our question is... How will the team handle it?"

Cash then turned to look at Dutch and Sandy before he looked at the others in the room. "We pay all of you enough that you should be able to figure out how to make this work to all of our benefit, right?"

Dutch Weingarten tossed a coffee cup against the wall, brown liquid painting the white space behind Cash's head. I turned to see he was okay, having ducked when he assessed the trajectory of Dutch's aim, but I was just fucking grateful he was alive. Dutch still had an arm, the old son of a bitch. I was about to go across the table after the asshole when Cash grabbed my arm and pulled me back into my seat.

There were witnesses to his outburst, so I skipped ahead, staring directly at Sandy to issue my question. He had been a straight shooter the entire time I'd known him, but if he had somehow changed, I had bystanders to back up my claim of discrimination due to our sexual orientation.

"Are you behind... Did you order someone to follow us and tape us? Did you suspect there was something more with us and decide it would hurt the team if it came out? Are you the one who is trying to blackmail us, or is it the organization?" I damn well wasn't letting that shit go.

I saw Dutch was completely surprised. "You can't possibly believe we would be behind something like that, can you? We... This will reflect badly on all of us, Brewer. We'd never try to hurt a player with such a promising future!" He'd gestured to Cash, just as I suspected.

I glanced to my left to see Cash tensing up, so I sat forward and braced my forearms on the table, leveling my stare at Sandy, who still hadn't said a word. "Here's our offer. We'll hold off on an official announcement."

I glanced at Gillian to confirm she hadn't released anything yet. When she nodded, I let go a held breath, grateful she had more business savvy than me. "And you'll hold off on any changes to the roster until the All-Star break. If we haven't proved to you that we have the team's best interests at heart, then send me down to Nashville to finish out this year and make Cash fight for his spot on the mound. You'd look awfully stupid if you sent him down now after the year he had. The rest of the team fucked up, which is why we didn't make it to the playoffs. Cash had nothing to do with the team's performance."

Sandy shook his head. "I'm sure they'd all be happy to hear

what you think of them, Brewer. So, if I'm hearing this right, this meeting stays within the confines of the people in this room? You won't announce your marriage, or even tell your teammates you got married, until the All-Star break? We have your word?"

I glanced at Cash to see a nod before he spoke. "Not a peep until the All-Star break, but if we're in the race for the pennant and possibly the World Series, you won't stop us from announcing our marriage?"

I saw Sandy and Dutch put their heads together, and I turned to look at my team, Josh and Gillian, and then noticed a sly smile on Luke's face, Cash's manager. He offered a covert nod before he reached into his briefcase and retrieved a folder. He opened it and began handing out stapled sets of papers to Sandy and Dutch. "I'll just remind you of Cash's contract before we get too far into this."

When Luke slid a copy to Cash, I saw the smug grin on my husband's handsome face. He quickly flipped to the page where the sticky note was attached, an arrow pointing to a highlighted paragraph that Cash pushed in front of me to read.

"The Memphis Blues organization agrees to waive any governance over the player's personal behavior, with the exception of any actions that constitute criminal conduct including, but not limited to, ..." the document outlined. As I read through the laundry list of exclusions, I was still stuck on the fact that anything pertaining to Cash's private life was off-limits. It was a damn good surprise. Somebody was a fucking genius.

"Who got this through?" I asked.

Cash leaned into my ear. "Uncle Skip negotiated it with Dorian Holt directly. Sandy showed up after they finished talking." I looked at him for confirmation I wasn't hearing things, and when he nodded, I wanted to roll on the floor laughing.

It had recently been speculated that Dorian Holt was the true owner of the Memphis Blues organization, not some fictitious entity as had been thought for the last few years. Holt was a bit of a hermit from what was reported in the media when the rumor first began to spread through the League.

There weren't any pictures of him anywhere and very little information on him other than his family owned Holt Industries, a multinational conglomerate with its fingers in more pies than anyone could count, and that Dorian had bought the team outside of Holt's control. It had been alleged that Dorian, an extremely young man in his late twenties, owned the whole thing, lock, stock and baseballs. I was a bit dumbstruck at the revelation Skip had actually met the man in person.

"How the fuck did Skip get a meeting with Dorian Holt?" The elusive owner of the Blues didn't attend the games as far as I knew. It was known among the team members that Dorian was the man who'd bought the team after the former owner had died five years earlier, leaving the team to his family, who didn't want it at all. Word on the street—or around the park—was that Dorian picked up the team for a song.

"Who fucking knows. Holt seemed like a nice guy. Good-looking, actually, and a lot younger than I expected. After everything was signed and my picture was taken wearing a Blues cap, Skip and Dorian Holt went out for dinner.

"I went back to the hotel and watched porn. I nearly ripped off my dick that night, because... Hell, have you seen Dorian Holt?" Cash wasn't kidding.

"As a matter of fact, nope. Has anyone ever seen him?" A thought struck, so I leaned closer. "Did you get a feel for the man? Will he hit the roof over this?"

Cash smirked. "I didn't even get to talk to him, but I'd bet Uncle Skip got a *real good* feel of him. I've never asked Kim what he knew about Uncle Skip's adventures, but Skip had alluded that he had lovers everywhere, and if I ever needed anything, I should let him know. He said he'd see if he had anyone nearby to help me. I just didn't know they were all men."

I nodded. "Well, okay. This should get some interest." I glanced around the room to see everyone reading the copies of Cash's contract that Luke had passed out. When I looked at Luke Schoenfeld, the large man winked at me.

Luke then rose from the table. "Okay, so how about we get through training camp first and then address *this* situation when the season starts. No disclosure by you guys, and no action by you guys?" Luke asked, glancing between us and Sandy and Dutch. Without waiting for an answer, Luke left the room.

I looked at Cash and extended my hand. "Shall we?"

Cash nodded, and the two of us left the conference room, hand in hand, before we walked down the stairs to the second floor. I opened the door to our room and let us in, not surprised to see two queen beds and our luggage on racks at the end of each.

I turned to Cash and decided to offer an incentive to get that fucking changeup where he needed it to be. We had to prove ourselves, especially now, and I damn well didn't want to give Sandy or Dutch anything to bitch about. Besides, we were still waiting for Kim's guy to figure out who the fuck was trying to blackmail us. My people hadn't responded to the story, so it was just speculation at that point.

"We only sleep in the same bed and have sex after a three-game series. I have to stay fit, and that python between your legs isn't conducive to me performing at my best.

"Tonight, after dinner, we go to the field and practice your weaker pitches, Cash. I want you to have a long career, and that goddamn changeup is necessary to fulfill the goal. You can be the most valuable asset on the Blues roster, whether I'm there or not, but you have to have your pitches down cold."

Cash walked over to me and touched my cheek. "Okay. *But...* I want an exception. If I pitch a no-hitter, I get sex that night. It doesn't have to be anal, but I deserve a damn reward."

I pulled him closer. "I love you, baby. Yes, you'll get your rewards, starting tonight. We haven't started training yet, remember?"

That sexy laugh had me peeling off his clothes. The taste of him on my tongue was exactly what I needed.

CHAPTER FOURTEEN

CASH

Cary stood from his squatted position, and I could see he was pissed. "Come on, Mitchell! Slower, goddammit!"

That was the problem, though, wasn't it? I was proud of my slider... my fastball... my curve... my breaking ball... even my split-finger fastball. All of those pitches, I'd learned and honed to a fine art. The damn changeup pitch, however, I just couldn't get. It was so fucking connected to my fastball, and I wasn't able to slow it down.

It was six o'clock on the Saturday night before the last game of the preseason. Cary and I had been working fucking hard on the changeup pitch. I hadn't been consistent with it during the preseason, which was frustrating as hell, and I could see my husband was feeling it as well. He'd played earlier that day, so he was probably tired and sore, which made him a bit cranky.

"I... I'm trying, Brewer, but..."

Cary stood from behind home plate and took off the mask, walking toward me. When he arrived at the mound, he stared into my eyes and then offered a grin. "I've been going about this shit all wrong. Let's call it a night, yeah?"

I wasn't sure what he meant, but I was tired, and a shower sounded good. I nodded and followed him to the dugout for him to stow his gear. I sat down on the bench, reaching for a bottle of water I'd brought with me. "Can we have couple time now?"

Cary took off his shin guards and dropped them on the floor of the dugout before he walked over to me and sat down, taking my water bottle to have a drink. "Sure."

"Do you think this is a lost cause?" I asked, needing to hear he believed in me. I felt as if I was the densest fucker on the planet because I couldn't figure out how to open my mind to get that fucking pitch right. I'd never been able to master the changeup, and I blamed my high school coach.

"That fucking fastball is all you need, kid. You can ride that thing all the way to the majors. A lot of guys think they need a bunch of fancy shit—slider, curveball, changeup—but you have that amazing fastball, and that's what you need to concentrate on," Coach Patrick had offered. I believed him until I hit college. My college pitching coach, Coach Ray, insisted on a lot more than just the fastball, and I learned the other pitches, but I never could master the changeup.

"Babe, nothing about you is a lost cause. Let's go clean up and get room service. We can discuss this and figure out a solution together." Cary's smile was all I really needed.

I nodded and followed him across the campus to our hotel. We showered separately, and Cary ordered dinner for both of us—seared salmon on baby greens with green goddess dressing to share, and sirloin steaks with mixed vegetables for each of us.

I pulled on basketball shorts and relaxed against the headboard of my bed, turning on the cable sports network to see the rundown of what was happening with the other teams during spring training. Cary was fucking around with his phone, so I closed my eyes and listened to the reporter drone on about the LA Stars' new pitcher, Pedro Arenas, and his preseason stats.

"The Stars home opener will be against the Memphis Blues on April 2. It's going to be interesting to see Arenas and Cash Mitchell face off. Both of these young guys have had a great preseason, and I predict, if the Blues stay as tight as they've looked recently, they'll be in the hunt for the pennant."

"Not so fast, man. Arenas has a killer changeup that Mitchell doesn't have. He's been avoiding the pitch every time Cary Brewer signals it, so I'd wager there's a bit of tension between the two with Mitchell waving off Brewer's calls.

"The Blues front office has been quiet on that little dustup about that audiotape that surfaced in the off-season, alleging Cary Brewer was having an affair with an unknown guy, so it should be interesting to see how much game time Brewer sees during the season. Rumor has it he's considering retirement at the end of the season," another voice speculated.

I opened my eyes to see a shot of myself mid-pitch from last season. The other half of the screen was a picture of Pedro Arenas standing on the mound, talking to Adam Silver, the Stars' pitching coach. I was guessing it was the sports reporting world's way of creating a beef between Arenas and me to spice —or hype—things up, what with the season starting the next week.

I'd played against Arenas in Triple-A ball when I was in Nashville and he was in Oakland with the Meteors—the Stars' farm team—and I knew the kid had an arm. He also had a hell of a changeup. The realization he'd been brought up from Triple-A ball and now I'd be judged against him was a bit unsettling.

I glanced over to Cary to see him furiously pecking away at his phone. "What are you doing?"

"Hang on. Just one more minute." He held up his index finger, and a second later, his phone chimed. The smile that grew on his face warmed me from the inside out.

Cary walked over to my bed and flopped down, leaning against the headboard while he held up his phone. "You like this place?" I glanced at the screen to see a beautiful, sprawling ranch house with fenced fields, a swimming pool, and a few horses seeming to graze in the background.

"Where's that?" I asked as I took the device and began scrolling through what I believed was a real estate listing.

"It's in Germantown near Chaves. He knows the couple who are selling, and he said if we're interested, we need to get on it," Cary informed me.

I froze. "You didn't tell him about us, did you?" God, that would blow everything sky high. We'd given our word we'd keep shit on the D-L, and if he'd made the mistake of telling Chaves, we might be fucked.

Cary leaned forward and kissed my cheek before he messed up my wet hair. "No, kid. When I say 'we,' I mean 'me.' I don't think Andy Chaves will give a shit about us, but some of the guys probably will have a problem. They'll forget all about us until they see us together, which is why I think we should break your lease, and I'll put my place up for sale. We can move out to the country and have privacy. You have the condo in Miami for when I retire, so I can live there during the season. We won't see much of each other, but we'll make it work."

I was still a bit confused. "So, you'll buy the place, and we'll live there together?" I wanted to confirm my understanding of his proposal. We each had money, so it wasn't jealousy, really. I just wanted something that was *ours*.

Cary seemed to sense that I was uneasy about something, so he took the phone from me and tossed it on the bed before he pulled me to sit on his thighs, facing him. His strong hands touched my cheeks, his thumbs rubbing over them as he looked into my eyes, his bright blue ones seeming to sparkle.

"You listen to me, Cash Mitchell. Everything I have is yours. After the season, we'll go to a lawyer and get everything straightened out on paper. I love you, and we're going to build a life together. Don't doubt me now, baby." Cary pulled me forward and kissed my lips softly a few times before I took control and fluttered my tongue over his mouth. When he opened, I lapped inside, tasting him, wanting more.

Cary wrapped his arms around my waist and pulled me closer. I reached up and encircled his broad shoulders, rutting my hard erection against his. Being in Cary's arms took me to another place, and I damn well wanted to stay there. No agents, pitching coaches, threats of outing the two of us. My safe space.

Cary Brewer gently ended the kiss and pulled back, his eyes searching mine. "Never doubt me. The way we feel when we're together will get us through the bad times, and we'll celebrate the good times, no matter how small. Now, let's talk about that changeup…"

Thankfully, the knock on the door pushed that discussion from the foreground, but I knew it wouldn't be for long. I hopped up and opened the door to allow the room service waiter to push the cart inside. When he saw Cary sitting on the bed in a pair of loose shorts, he glanced at me and then at the other bed where Cary had been sleeping.

We'd tried to stick to our deal of no sex, but there were a few blow jobs and hand jobs that had crept in when we showered together. That had been my fault because I would get in with him without his permission, but I wasn't a damn bit sorry about it.

"If I could get your signature?" the kid asked, holding out a black folio. I flipped it open and signed the check, and Cary walked over and gave the kid a bill I didn't see, but when the guy's face lit up with a splitting grin, I knew my man had been generous.

"Thank you, guys. If you need anything, just call the front desk and ask for Joe Robalos." I looked at the young man's face to see a sweet smile, and it made me happy.

I was feeling all gooey from love, so I decided to be generous. "You off tomorrow? We've got the noon game, and I can get you two tickets if you want."

"*Wow*! That would be great. I'll bring my boyfriend. He thinks you're sexy, Mr. Brewer," the kid explained. I turned to see that cocky grin on Cary's face, and I laughed.

"Your boyfriend has good taste," Cary added before he grabbed his phone and sent a text. He looked up at the guy. "Your tickets are at will-call under Robalos. Have fun. Bring your boyfriend down for autographs after the game. I'll sign something for him."

I turned to look at my husband and smirked. "You cocky fucker."

Our companion giggled, thanked us again, and left the room—which was suddenly filled with sexual tension. I didn't know if the kid could sense it, but my body was like the wick on a stick of dynamite, just sizzling toward an explosion.

Cary lifted the lids on the three dishes and then picked up the salmon salad and went to sit on my bed again, leaning against the headboard. I went to the fridge, which had been stripped of anything but juice and water, and I grabbed two bottles of water before I went to join him on the bed. As I was about to settle next to him, he put the plate on the nightstand.

"Nope. On my lap. We're going to talk about what's going through your head when you're getting ready to throw the changeup. So, what goes through your head?" I chortled at his approach.

Cary picked up the plate and held a bite of the salad up to my mouth, watching me closely. I closed my lips around the tines of the fork and slid the food into my mouth. The salmon was sort of sweet, and then the heat started to tickle my tongue.

"Damn, that's really good. Have you had it before?" The previous year when we were at training camp, I'd shared a room with a kid from NC State who was there for a spot on the Blue Notes as an outfielder. Poor kid got hurt the second day of practice and went home, leaving me with a room to myself. I ate hamburgers every night.

"Yeah. This is what grown-ups eat. You've got a hot body and a young metabolism. Just wait a few years. Everything slows down and heads south... even your balls," Cary told me before eating some of the salad and then feeding me another bite.

I thought about his request as I chewed. It was Coach Ray's voice I heard every time I saw the sign for the changeup. *"You suck at it. Your mind is fucking with you, and you need to learn to get over it."*

We finished the salmon salad and then I climbed off his lap and grabbed the other dishes, placing them on the small round table, along with utensils. Cary got up from the bed and came over, pulling out the chair across from me. "What's in your head?" he asked again.

I took the dome off my plate, seeing the steak looked delicious, and even the steamed broccoli and cauliflower didn't look bad. I salted the vegetables and forked a floret, ready to put it in my mouth when Cary said, "Broccoli, cauliflower, asparagus. All vegetables that make your spunk taste bad. Neither of us wants to taste it, so we won't be trading blow jobs.

"Now, tell me what pops in your head when you see my

signal—and, by the way, if you keep waving off my signals, I'll take it out on your ass when I get you home."

I swallowed the food in my mouth before I cracked up. Cary Brewer would never be able to compartmentalize our personal relationship from our professional one. I found I didn't want him to, either.

CHAPTER FIFTEEN

CARY

I let Cash eat in peace, seeing he was trying to give me an answer for what went through his head when I signaled the changeup pitch. The kid was like a perfectly calibrated sniper rifle with every other pitch he threw, and he could put the perfect spin on a breaking ball like it was a goddamn top. The reason he couldn't slow that changeup was a mental block, and we were going to figure it out. I'd resort to less than ethical means to do it without any hesitation.

When Cash placed his knife and fork on his plate, I put the dome over my unfinished meal and placed both of our plates on the room service cart before shoving it out in the hallway and locking up for the night. It was almost eight, so I figured if we were asleep by ten, we could get a solid eight and be at the park for batting practice by nine.

Cash was starting the last game of the preseason, and I wanted to break through whatever barrier was between him and that changeup, and I thought I had the perfect way to do it.

"On the bed. Shorts off," I demanded before I went to the bathroom to wash my hands and grab the lube. We kept it in the shower because I was able to entice Cash to shower with me in the morning, especially if I made him think I was against it. I loved it when he thought he got his way. He was anxious to get his prize—my cock in his mouth. It was the old win-win!

"Seriously? I just ate, Cary!"

Of course, I laughed. I'd only eaten a third of my steak, though I did eat the veggies. My young husband was still a growing boy, and he needed his protein. Besides, I planned to feed him plenty of fruit to sweeten up his spunk. I loved tasting him on my tongue.

I returned to the bedroom and tossed the lube on the bed. "No condom?" Cash's voice was raspy, which gave away how torqued up he was. His cock was hard, and his hand was stroking it, which needed to stop.

"Hands off. Legally, it's mine now. So, you've had about thirty minutes to think about it—tell me what goes through your head when you see the signal to throw a changeup?"

I saw Cash's face flush, and he started biting on his lip, which was a tell that he was getting upset. I stepped over to the bed and sat down on the side, placing my hand on Cash's thigh. "You know anything you tell me goes no further. I love you, Cash. Nothing you can say will change that." I was trying to be reassuring. I felt that was important under the circumstances.

Cash swallowed, his eyes not meeting mine, so I stood, sliding my shorts off, and lay down next to him, my hand over his heart. Cash finally looked at me. "It's stupid, really. It's just that every time you signal the changeup, I think about my high school coach. I hear his voice in my head telling me that speed is the key, and it goes against my instincts to slow the pitch. *'All you need is a fastball,'* he'd say, and it's ingrained in my soul.

"When I went to college, Coach Ray told me I'd never get anywhere without learning how to throw the other pitches, and he asked how the fuck I even made it to college without them. I lost my confidence, and I couldn't hit the broadside of a barn that whole year.

"Uncle Skip took the summer off and worked with me. The only pitch I couldn't get down is the fucking changeup. Uncle Skip tried everything he knew, and he couldn't get me out of it. I just... I froze every time that damn pitch was signaled. It doesn't make sense, really," Cary explained.

I was no psychiatrist, but I could see the kid had to have something else to think about when I signaled the changeup, so it was my plan to do just that.

I reached for the lube and flipped the cap. "You know, there are occasions when slower is better." I squeezed some in my right palm and closed my hand to warm it a little. "I mean, you wouldn't drive a car fast all the time. You'd get stopped for speeding, and you'd likely run over a few people, wouldn't you?"

I gently ran a slick finger up Cash's flaccid dick, slowly circling the head before running my finger down it again, feeling it firm up at my touch. "Now, you wouldn't want me to do this fast, would you?"

I propped my clean hand under my head and stared into Cash's beautiful eyes, seeing I had his undivided attention. "I mean, sometimes it's better to slow things down so you can savor them, don't you think?"

I ghosted my lips over Cash's neck and wrapped the rest of my fingers around his now stiff dick, slowly gliding my fist up and down a couple of times before I opened my hand and slid my slick finger down behind his balls to his taint where I slowly moved my finger, applying just a little pressure.

"Oh, *fuck!*" His eyes had closed until I pressed a bit harder on his skin and then moved further back to his pucker, slowly circling my slick finger.

"I want you to think about how good a slow finger feels

rubbing all those nerve endings around your pretty hole. You know something I'd love to do to you? I'd love to eat your ass. I bet it's better than that steak we just had. Now, if I was going to eat your ass and tongue fuck you, you wouldn't want me to do it fast, would you? You'd want me to go slow and long.

"We're going to change the signal for the changeup. When I put my middle finger on my pants over my hole, I want you to think about how slow you want me to eat that fucking ass. I want you to think about how slow you want to slide your cock inside me and show me who I belong to for the rest of my life."

I moved my hand back to Cash's rod, seeing the head was engorged and purple, just as I wanted it to be. I hated the idea of what I was going to do to him; I had to try something a bit drastic. I gave him two more slow pulls and swirled my tongue over his stubbled cheek before I stopped everything and got out of bed, my hard cock throbbing as I walked away.

"What the fuck!" Cash gasped.

I laughed as I closed and *locked* the bathroom door, turning on the shower as cold as it would go. I stepped under the water, feeling the frigid spray take my breath. I wasn't going to let my man suffer alone. His dick was mine, and I wanted to celebrate the win with it inside me. That changeup would be the surprise of a lifetime for the first batter at my home plate. I couldn't wait!

"I'm not ready, so don't signal it!" Cash was in a bitchy mood, and of course, it was my fault. I was standing outside the batting cage while Cash was taking batting practice, and he was so much on edge, I pitied the asshole who set him off.

"Well, well. Look who it is—the Memphis Belles!" I turned

to see the last fucking thing I wanted to see—Jeff Quattlebaum strolling out on the field with that fuckhead, Nick Gregson.

I stepped toward them to see what the fuck they were doing on the field when we had a game to play in two hours. "Quattlebaum. Gregson. What brings you boys by? Interested to see how a winning team prepares for a game?"

Quattlebaum stepped to me with a smug grin on his face. "Roger called me. Seems you and your little bitch are on the way out when you lose today. He asked that we come to the game so Nick can be ready to go back to Memphis with the team. Nick's going to start on Tuesday after your boy and his nonexistent changeup blow the game today.

"What I can't figure out is how you got out of that fucking audiotape bullshit. Nick caught you two in that goddamn bathroom, and somebody was sucking somebody's dick. Nick called Roger to come down and tried to get a picture of you guys, but Roger told him to get back to his room before Dutch did bed check and not to say a word about you and Mitchell.

"You made enemies on the team, Brewer, when you backed Skip's play to bring his fucking nephew up from the farm team. Roger was the one who got you guys on tape when Mitchell was blowing you—or that's what it sounded like to us when we listened to it. Unfortunately, without pictures, it wasn't as effective as we'd hoped. Now, though, when the story hits the wire that you two fags got married? Yeah, that's gonna go over like a lead balloon. I know all about it!

"Nobody in the fucking league will want a damn thing to do with you two butt pirates, so enjoy it while you can. That job you think you have with the Sharks? Yeah, I heard about it, and I can promise you it will disappear like a donut at a police station.

"We couldn't get you in the press because only those idiots on one of the gossip sites would run it without proof and Roger didn't get a picture of the two of you, but I could damn well go behind the scenes and skewer any shot you have of working in baseball again," Quattlebaum threatened.

I nodded. "Yeah, I guess you got me. Uh, was Roger in on this with you?"

Quattlebaum laughed. "You bet. He wants Nick on the team and your bitch gone. He's been looking for any reason to dump Mitchell, and now he's got it. When the kid gets pulled from the game after the first inning, you'll hear that sweet flushing sound of Mitchell's career going down the shitter. I sure as fuck can't wait!"

Roger Fucking Hardy! Cash's pitching coach was the person who taped us, and that led me to believe the whole fucking clubhouse was in on it. In my mind, all fucking promises were down the shitter as well.

I started toward the locker room because I was going to beat the living fuck out of Roger Hardy, that little cunt. "*Cary! Cary Brewer!*"

I turned to look over my shoulder to see Kimber Donlyn with his friends, Manny, Benny, and Keith. A very large man was standing with his arm around Manny, and all of them were smiling.

I walked over to the fence to greet them. "Hey, guys! I know Cash will be happy to see you here. He's nervous, so knowing you guys are here to support him will really give him something to worry about." I shook hands with them as we all had a chuckle at Cash's expense.

The big guy shook my hand before handing me a file. "I'm London St. Michael. I believe this is what you've been looking for."

I took the folder and opened it, seeing a stapled set of papers. I began reading, and the information contained in the document could have been helpful a few minutes earlier. It confirmed Roger Hardy was the culprit behind the audio clip released by that shithead gossip site, GSPOT.

What I didn't know was that Hardy's stepson worked at GSPOT, but that just added more fuel to my fire to get to Hardy and kick his ass. When I flipped the paper, there was a picture of Hardy, but the woman he was snuggled up with wasn't his wife, Andrea. I'd met her at team functions, and she was a very nice lady.

"That's Gina Vaguyna. She works the drag circuit on the East Coast. That particular picture was taken at BOYS! BOYS! BOYS! in Key West. The next one is at Pipe Fitters in Pittsburgh, and the next one is at Club One in Savannah, Georgia. Seems Roger Hardy has a dirty little secret," Kim informed.

"I talked to Gina's alter ego, Aaron Miles, who lives outside of Memphis, and he identified Roger as a guy he's fuck buddies with. The dates for the pictures I was able to get off social media, thanks to my buddy the hacker, coincide with games from last season. Seems Roger would go in advance..."

"To make sure everything was ready for the team's arrival the next day," I supplied, seeing it all clearly for the first time.

"Cary, Gina is set to perform at a club in town tonight, Dance Mesa. They host a drag show every Sunday night, and Gina's the headliner. That seems a little convenient, doesn't it? You want us to go to see if Roger Hardy makes an appearance?" Kim had the most wicked look on his face. I wanted to kiss him, but then I had a better idea.

"No, but you guys go ahead and report back. You guys got your tickets for the game?" I'd buy them tickets if they didn't. I wanted Cash to know he had family there to see him.

"Yes, we do, and guess who's coming to join us? Carole!" Kim informed. I had a chill run down my spine, but no time like the present to officially meet my mother-in-law.

"Great! I have a surprise for Cash, so pay close attention!" I shook hands again with them and booked it to the locker room, seeing Cash was no longer practicing. I walked back to his locker where Roger was talking to him, and I immediately saw red.

"Look, Mitchell, if you don't want an anonymous source to come up with your marriage license, do you?"

That was it. I started for Roger, but Cash got him first, busting the motherfucker in the mouth. I saw Roger's nose was bleeding, which made me smile, but then I saw Cash cradling his left hand.

I quickly hopped the bench to get to him. "What the fuck did you do?"

"It's broken, but I don't care. Get Whitey to tape it up, and let's get on with it," Cash snapped. I could see the adrenaline was coursing through his veins like white-water rapids, and I knew he didn't feel anything.

"Ba-Buddy, I think you need a doctor, not a trainer." I stammered out, correcting the pet name I was about to use when I noticed a bunch of the guys standing around to see what had happened.

Whitey Black was the team trainer, a trained paramedic in the off-season. I knew Whitey was good with most things, but I wasn't sure he could deal with Cash's broken hand. Thank god he'd used his left and not his pitching hand. That could have ended his career.

"It's fine. I'm gonna pitch this game, Brewer. Now, find Whitey and tell him to get in here. I've got a game to win."

I could see his mind was made up, and it *was* his catching hand. If it was wrapped, hopefully it wouldn't do more damage. I headed out of the clubhouse and over to the dugout where Whitey was checking supplies. "Mitchell needs you in the clubhouse," I stated as I saw Dutch coming around the corner in a hell of a hurry.

"Brewer! What the fuck..." He seemed to notice people were looking at him, so Dutch stopped yelling and rushed over to the dugout.

"What?" I asked as innocently as possible.

Dutch slapped me in the chest with a priority mail envelope. "Don't have your fucking mail delivered to the front office. What the fuck happened between Roger and Mitchell? Chavez said Mitchell punched Roger in the nose?"

We might have a brawl before the fucking game ever started. "Did you tell Roger Hardy that Cash and I got married?" I stepped close enough to Dutch that his gut was against mine. I might end up breaking my fucking hand as well.

I saw Dutch's face flush, which meant one of two things—he was embarrassed he got caught, or he was pissed that I was confronting him with such an accusation. Dutch stepped back and shook his head. "I... I was just... We were in the head, and I made a joke about hangin' out a rainbow flag and singin' YMCA instead of the National Anthem. He laughed and asked what I was talking about, and I said we had newlyweds in our midst before I even thought about it.

"I'm sorry, Brewer. I shut up as soon as I realized what I said, okay? It won't happen again," Dutch vowed.

That wasn't good enough, but I had another question. "Did you tell Roger to get that Gregson shit here to fly home with the team?" I was about to rip someone limb from limb. I needed to get a handle on my mood because I seriously doubted my groom wanted to visit me in lockup.

"No! I hate that little shit. He couldn't lick Mitchell's cleats. Come to think of it, Lou Clayton mentioned the kid the other day and said we should give him another tryout. I knew Roger was hot on the kid because he's a southpaw, but we don't need him. He's a glory hog," Dutch complained. I nodded, but I wasn't ready to let any of those fucks off the hook.

"I want Rico Suarez brought up to work with Cash. I am retiring at the end of the season, and I want Rico to take my place. Don't go looking for a catcher. You've got a great one in Nashville. I wanna work with him before I leave," I insisted.

"Why would you leave?"

"Because queers aren't welcome here," I reminded him as I turned away, done with him.

I glanced around the park to see news cameras and sports networks had set up to broadcast the game, and I had an idea. I was probably going to hell, and Cash might never sleep with me again, but it was a chance I was willing to take.

CHAPTER SIXTEEN

CASH

My fucking hand was throbbing, but I could block it out. I was so fucking mad at Roger Hardy, he was lucky I was set to pitch that day, or I'd have hit him with my right fist and knocked the fucker out.

Whitey gave me a cortisone shot to get me through the game, and he iced it, having wrapped it so I could still wear my glove. He'd warned me that I needed X-rays, but I blew him off and walked away with a "thanks." I went to my locker, happy to see that fucker Hardy wasn't still lying on the floor, and I proceeded to finish getting dressed for the game.

Cary came into the clubhouse with a priority mail envelope in his grip and a big smile on his face. He tore it open and spilled something out of it into his hand. He then looked around before he quickly reached into his locker for something else and walked into the bathroom.

I had no fucking idea what he'd been doing after he sent Whitey in to look at my hand, but I needed to get my goddamn mind on the game. I reached for my phone and earbuds on the shelf of my locker and put the buds in my ears, hitting my

"Pump Up" playlist—old-school rock and rap—and I sat down with my cap over my eyes, ignoring the rest of the activity around me.

I went through the pitches in my head, feeling my muscles tighten and release as my body prepared for battle. The music pumped me up, and I could feel the synapses zapping in my brain until I got to the fucking changeup pitch. That fucking thing was killing me until I heard Cary's voice in my head.

"You know, there are occasions when slower is better."

He had that low growl sometimes that had my cock weeping when it probably shouldn't have been.

"I mean, you wouldn't drive a car fast all the time. You'd get stopped for speeding, and you'd likely run over a few people, wouldn't you?"

The memory of his index finger, slick with lube, trailing up my soft cock nearly took away my breath. It was totally unexpected, but it was more than welcome.

"Now, you wouldn't want me to do this fast, would you?"

The memory of Cary's slick fingers teasing my dick. His calloused hands caressing my body and his tongue swirling on my cheek had my rod springing to life in my jock, which sure as fuck wasn't comfortable.

"I want you to think about how good a slow finger feels rubbing all those nerve endings around your pretty hole. You know something I'd love to do to you? I'd love to eat your ass. I bet it's better than that steak we just had. Now, if I was going to eat your ass and tongue fuck you, you wouldn't want me to do it fast, would you? You'd want me to go slow and long."

Oh, god...

"We're going to change the signal for the changeup. When I put my middle finger on my pants over my hole, I want you to think about how slow you want me to eat that fucking ass. I

want you to think about how slow you want to slide your cock inside me and show me who I belong to for the rest of my life."

I had to stop thinking about those things or I'd need to go rub one out in the john. I felt a foot tapping against my outstretched legs, and I opened my eyes to see Cary standing next to me with his sexy smile. "Would you like to join me in the bullpen, or are you meditating, Mitchell?"

I chuckled and took out my earbuds as I stood and grabbed my jacket to take to the dugout. "Hey, you didn't ask me to change my name. Why?" I asked as we walked out of the clubhouse and headed toward the field.

"I'm not particularly proud of my name. My parents were drug addicts and burned down the house with my little brother in it because they were cooking meth. There's no fame associated with the Brewer name," Cary stated, surprising the hell out of me.

I stopped him, touching his arm. "What? How did I not..."

He turned to me and smiled. "Mitchell, not the time. We have the rest of our lives." Well, he was right on that count.

We went to the dugout, and I hung my jacket on the hook and slid my phone and earbuds into the pocket, grabbing my glove from the end of the bench and sitting down as Cary put on his gear.

"I know a secret," he chanted in singsong fashion.

I chuckled as I took a paper cup to fill it with Gatorade. "Hints?" I asked, remembering the banter we'd had the previous year when we didn't know each other very well, and Cary was trying to calm me down before a game when I was starting.

"Uh, people who love you are here," he offered as he buckled his shinpads.

I laughed. "You?"

"I said 'people,' not the most important person in your life. Two more guesses."

"I damn well know it's not Roger," I stated as I saw the bastard make his way across the field to the bullpen, signaling I should head over to warm up.

"Uh, I have no fucking idea. I need to get to the bullpen. Are you coming over?"

"I'm not, and neither are you. We're going to warm up on the field. Kim and the queens are here along with a big bastard who seems to like Manny," Cary admitted as he pulled on his chest pad. He turned around, and I buckled the sides for him. It was just routine.

Hearing family was there was a surprise. "Where?" I asked as I glanced out at the stadium seating. The seats were filling up, and I was glad, but I couldn't see my people.

Cary walked over to me and whispered, "They love you. They brought a guest who we'll see after the game, so let's win this, okay? We have a lot riding on it, so are you ready?"

I took a breath and exhaled, looking into Cary's beautiful blue eyes. "I'm ready. I love you, by the way."

He turned that sexy grin my way, and I melted. "Yeah, you do."

Cary Brewer stepped out of the dugout, and the crowd roared. He had a reputation as a fierce catcher, protecting his plate like it was his most beloved possession. I'd seen him hit a batter who encroached on the plate, and I had learned how to help him protect that prime real estate.

I watched him wave to the crowd as he walked out to his post, a gladiator preparing for battle. I waited for the cheers to calm, and then I stepped out of the dugout, shocked to hear the cheers for me. I looked around to see if I could spot Kim and company, but the stadium had filled completely. Hearing people I didn't know shouting my name sort of took my breath every time the sound reached my ears. When I saw Cary clapping his hands over his head to encourage the crowd, my heart skipped a beat.

I took the mound and followed the signals Cary gave me to warm up. There was music playing over the speaker system, and it drowned out the crowd, which let me get lost in my head.

Five pitches—a fastball... a curveball... another fastball... a breaking ball, left... a knuckleball... Cary took off his mask and smiled at me, giving me the thumbs-up that we were okay and ready to win.

I jogged off the field to the dugout for all the ceremonial shit with the National Anthem and the honor guard. We all stood on the sidelines and held our hands over our hearts like good patriots. Once the flag-waving was finished, a young man who had won a citizenship award for spearheading a food drive in his community in Mesa threw out the first pitch, and Cary chased it down. He ran to the mound and hugged the kid, giving him the ball and saying something to him that made the kid grin.

The kid ran off the field, holding the baseball Cary had given him and looking very happy. I stepped out of the dugout and walked out to the mound. The umpire gave Cary a ball, and he started toward the mound with it, his catcher's mask resting on top of his head with a big grin on his face.

I stepped on the mound and reached for the rosin bag, tossing it in the air a few times with my right hand. My left was hidden in my glove because I damn well didn't want to show the public my stupidity from earlier in the day.

The rally music was playing as we were preparing to warm up, and Cary jogged up to the mound with the game ball. "Brewer, nice job."

Cary smirked. "I know. I'm good with kids. So, uh, your mom is here, by the way. I asked them all to stick around so we can take them out after the game. So, those pitches were great. You ready for this?"

I took the ball and tossed it in the air, winking at the man. "It's our job, right?"

"Yeah, but it's not our life, right?"

"Well, no, but it's where we make our money," I reminded him, tossing the ball in the air again.

"Buckle up," Cary said as he reached under his game jersey and pulled out a chain with one of the shitty silver rings attached. He slipped it over my neck and smiled. "I've got our wedding bands in the safe in the room. These are the fantastic rings you bought us."

I laughed at him as he put it over my neck. I picked it up and saw the same ring hanging off his neck as well. "Pucker up, baby," Cary stated before he tossed off his catcher's mask and took my face in his hands, kissing me with everything inside him.

I started to pull away, but when Cary Brewer's tongue found its way inside my mouth, I found I didn't give a flying fuck! Our tongues swirled, and I could hear cheers from the crowd along with boos. When Cary pulled away and looked at me, he smiled. "We're officially out, baby. I love you. Let's do this shit!"

I laughed as he jogged back to home plate, and I got my mind right where it needed to be. We were heading into the season, and I wanted to look down that field and see Cary Brewer with that catcher's mitt ready to take what I was throwing.

Cary held his middle finger over his hole, and I knew what he wanted from me, but I waved him off. Of course, he wasn't having that. Cary whipped off his mask and held his hands up in a T before he ran out to the mound.

"Mitchell, I refuse to suck your cock or eat your ass unless you try it. This next bastard coming up won't expect the changeup. *Do not* wave me off again. I will fucking make you pay," he snapped at me from behind his glove.

I chuckled and nodded. "Okay, let's see what happens."

What I didn't expect was for Roger Hardy to come out and step to the mound. "Are we playing the game?"

Cary turned on him. "You and Lou put this shit together that you were going to bring up Nick Gregson. Fuck you, Roger."

That was news to me. "Wait, what?"

"We have a game. Can we play it and take this up later?" Cary asked as he stared at Roger. I nodded and stepped away. Cary jogged back to home plate, and Roger headed back to the bullpen.

I stood on the mound and closed my eyes, knowing what was coming. Cary was going to push me for that fucking pitch, and I wasn't going to let him down.

When I saw Cary put his middle finger near his ass, I closed my eyes and remembered what he'd told me. *"You know, there are occasions when slower is better."*

I took a deep breath, and I nodded at him, seeing his smirk. I cocked the gun, and I fired. When I saw that ball spiraling at a slower trajectory than usual toward Cary's mitt, I held my breath. The *swoosh* of the bat was surprising. The loud *smack* of the ball against Cary's glove and *"Strike!"* yelled out from the ump was like time slowed for not only that ball, but for me as well. I opened my eyes to see the ball had hit its mark.

Cary stood and threw the ball back to me more gently than usual—likely because he remembered my hand—before he made kissy lips at me after lifting the face mask, so I nodded and walked off the mound. I wound my arm a bit to loosen up, knowing full and well that Cary was going to call for that changeup again.

I stepped back to the mound as he took his stance and nodded. He held his middle finger to his ass again, and I nodded. I took a deep breath and cleared my mind, visualizing that pitch again and rejoicing when the sound of leather against leather reverberated in the park as the ball hit Cary's glove.

I quickly got lost in the game, and seven innings later, Dutch walked out to the mound. Cary jogged up, handing me the ball and touching the end of his mitt to the face mask to hide any comments he might make the other team.

Dutch looked between us before studying me. "Kid, are you tired? You're at a no-hitter. I'll leave this shit up to you. Oh, I'm firing Roger and Lou as soon as the game ends. Those two assholes should have been gone a long time ago. So?"

I glanced at Cary, who had a smirk on his handsome face, making me grin. "I'm good. Can I keep going? Brewer owes me something, and I really want it." I looked at my husband, seeing pink cheeks and that sexy smile he saved for me.

Damn! It was gonna be a fine life!

EPILOGUE
CASH

One year later...

I was standing at the bar waiting for Cary's and my drink while he was talking to Lou Martino, the general manager for the Chicago Breeze, in the corner of the ballroom. There was a touch to my shoulder, and when I turned, I was surprised to see Randi Counts, a reporter with SportsNet Cable Sports Network. She was a lovely woman, and I was happy to see her again. The last time we'd spent time together was a day about a year before that I'd never forget.

"No comment."

It was a joke, because at Cary's insistence, we'd given her the exclusive interview after that spectacular kiss on the mound in the last game of preseason that had gotten us nominated for "Can't-Stop-Watching Moment of the Year" at the ESPY Awards. I was sure neither Cary nor I wanted to win the damn thing, but that kiss had gone viral. Surprisingly, the front office hadn't really caused a ruckus after the SportsNet did a weeklong series on being gay in professional sports.

Lou Clayton and Roger Hardy had both been sacked in the middle of the game, and Dutch had actually brought Sonny Rhimes up from Nashville the day of the interview, which had me thrilled. I'd worked with Sonny the year I played for the Blue Notes, and the two of us got along famously. He didn't ride me about that changeup back then, and when he saw I finally got my shit together and perfected the pitch, it earned me high praise from the man who reminded me an awful lot of Uncle Skip. I looked up to him, so that made me feel good.

Randi ordered a glass of wine when my drinks were delivered, and I stepped aside so she could have the chair I was standing behind. After Randi was seated, she turned to smile at me. "So, how's married life? How long is it?"

"How long will I be on injured reserve?" I held up my left hand that was still in a brace. I'd had some nerve damage repaired in my left hand after breaking it when I punched Roger Hardy before that fateful game. The team ended up making a deal with him to give him a bonus and say he'd left the team for personal reasons as long as he didn't file charges against me. I paid a hefty fine for my behavior, but the team donated it to a women's and children's shelter in town, and that made me happy.

It was July, and I was expected to begin working out with the team later in the month. I was antsy to get back to work.

"No, Mitchell. How long since you and Brewer moved into the solitude of your dude ranch outside of Memphis? Family in the works?" Randi asked.

I chuckled. "As I said, no comment, but off the record, we moved after Thanksgiving. We went to Florida to be with family, and then we wrangled them to come back with us and help us move. You should come out for a weekend. We've got a few horses and some beautiful trails to ride," I invited. I really did like her. She had been good to us with that interview.

"Good evening. I'm Randi Counts, and I'm here in the locker room—no-woman's land, according to a lot of men. I'm with Cary Brewer, starting catcher for the Memphis Blues. Cary, would you like to introduce my other guest?"

From there, it was a forty-five-minute interview, and we hadn't made any topics off-limits to Randi. Our team—our agents and publicist—and our *team*, as in the Memphis Blues, joined us behind the scenes offering their support. It was honestly one of the best days of my life. There were a few questions that brought nervous giggles from the peanut gallery, but to us, it was no more uncomfortable than a prostate exam—which we performed on each other as often as possible.

"Hey, I'm up for two awards for that series. You guys want to go with me to the ceremonies? Two handsome dates would be much more impressive than one," Randi invited. Her drink was delivered, and then she turned to face me, but I only had eyes for the man heading in our direction. My husband looked damn good in a tuxedo.

"Sorry, Cash. Lou was interested in what I'm going to do after I nurse you back to health." Cary leaned forward and kissed Randi on each cheek before he took his drink from my hand, pecking my cheek for making the run so he could have privacy with Martino.

I was tempted to ask Cary *exactly* what Martino wanted, but not in front of a reporter. Cary had taken time off after the World Series to help me through the bullshit of surgery and rehab, but I could tell he was itching to get back to work as much as me.

"Randi asked if we'd like to escort her to two award ceremonies," I informed him, studying Cary's face to see it smush up in disgust as I expected.

"Not for anything." Randi and I both started cackling at his response, which was just what I expected.

The lights dimmed twice, so Cary extended his arm to Randi. "How about we just escort you to your seat, beautiful?" Randi nodded and showed him her ticket. I followed behind them, and after Randi was seated, we went over to our row, taking our places next to Dutch and Sonny.

Nobody else on the team was up for any awards, and Gillian had strongly urged us to go to Los Angeles for the ceremony to show the world we weren't ashamed or embarrassed about our marriage and were excited about our future. Much against either of our better judgment, there we were.

We clapped for the winners and listened to the speeches, though both of us were on our phones with each other so we weren't caught talking on camera.

Cary: You look hot in that tuxedo. What are you wearing under it?

Me: Who says I'm wearing anything?

Cary: Don't tease. Remember that garter belt and thong Kim gave me?

Me: You're trying to kill me, aren't you?

Cary: Never, Pitcher. I got a call from Dorian Holt this afternoon while you were getting a haircut.

Me: Really? What did he want?

Cary: He's coming to Memphis next week. He wants to talk to me.

I glanced up to him and saw a wink, which had the potential to be good news. I didn't want to leave our beautiful home behind, but if Cary had to go somewhere else for his job because he'd officially retired after the Series, then we'd work it out.

Me: Whatever you want to do, you know I support you.

Cary reached over and took my hand, resting his phone on his lap as we watched the ceremony for a bit.

As much as I didn't want to be there, I was with the man I loved, and that made it okay. I would walk through hellfire for that man without question. The beauty of feeling that way—I knew he'd do the same for me. I'd never felt surer of anything in my life than I was that Cary Brewer was meant for me.

The biggest mystery that would never be solved was how did my Uncle Skip know it? I'd be eternally grateful for him and his insight, and for all of the love he shared with the people who mattered to him. It was a beautiful thing.

CARY

For the first time in my life, I had stage fright. I stood on that stage after it was announced that we won that stupid award, holding on to Cash like a lifeline. Not surprisingly, my love sensed I couldn't speak, so he stepped to the mic like the champ he'd show everyone he could be.

"Wow! We certainly didn't expect that moment on the mound would cause such a stir, but for me, it was one of the most beautiful things that has ever happened. I have to give credit to my late uncle, Skip Mitchell, for guiding me to Cary."

The applause sort of snapped me out of it, and I turned to look at Cash—my sweet, kind, beautiful husband, who didn't have one fake bone in his body. He was my heart, and I hadn't started to think mushy shit like that until I met the man during spring training.

Cash spoke for another minute about how great the year had been for the whole team and how much he was looking forward to finishing physical therapy and going back to play for the Blues. The applause was a welcome surprise. Cash then stepped aside, motioning for me to step forward and speak. I laughed nervously before I cleared my throat. "My life is a freakin' miracle. Skip Mitchell and I met years ago when he'd scouted me during my college years in Michigan.

"Skip brought me to the attention of the Miami Sharks, and when I got called up from Triple-A ball, Skip was like an uncle to me as well. He was always only a phone call away when I needed someone to talk to, and I'll always be grateful for him.

"I had no idea this fantastic guy was coming my way, and I'm truly blessed. Skip called me a few times and kept me in the loop about his nephew's ball career. Cash was a rising star with an arm like a rocket, and Skip sent me game film from his games so I could see it for myself. It sounds ridiculous, I know, but after I met Cash at training camp, everything in my life just seemed to fall into place, and I still see it as a miracle.

"The day that kiss took place, a lot of things had happened. When Cash was warming up, we had a bit of a disagreement about some signals we needed to clarify, so I walked out to the mound, and as I stood there, I knew I was a lucky son of a bitch.

"So, this award is dedicated to a man everyone loved. This is for you, Skip! Thank you!"

I turned to Cash and grinned. "Pucker up, baby."

I kissed him, hearing the cheers from the crowd, which felt good. I knew I wouldn't always hear cheers when I kissed my husband, but it didn't matter. I had what was best for me, and I would be forever grateful.

We walked off the stage, and I pulled him out of the venue into a warm Los Angeles night. I held up my arm to hail a cab and turned to Cash. "Remember that garter belt, hose, and thong Kim gave me? I'm wearing it under my tux. You didn't ask, but I thought you should know."

A cab stopped, and I pushed Cash toward the curb, seeing his glazed-over eyes, just as I'd hoped.

Skip Mitchell had done me the greatest favor I'd never asked him to do—he brought me to the man who would be my future.

Later that night, I'd planned to tell Cash I was going to be offered the job of the new bullpen coach for the Memphis Blues, having turned down Lou Martino's offer at the party because Dutch had given me a head's up that Dorian Holt wanted me for the job. My husband had a great future, and I was damn sure going to be front and center to witness it, by his side. Always, by his side.

**If you enjoyed "Cash & Cary," please drop by and leave a review
on Amazon, Goodreads, or BookBub.**

**"Kim & Skip" is the prequel to "Cash & Cary," and the novella is currently available for pre-order on Amazon. It's on sale for 99¢ until it's release on June 25! Get your copy now.
mybook.to/Kim_and_Skip.
Want more from "Cash & Cary?" How about the interview scene? Download the exclusive short for free! Bonus Scene for Cash & Cary**

Thank you for reading!

ABOUT THE AUTHOR

I am proud to say I grew up in the rural Midwest until I was fortunate enough to meet a dashing young man who swept me off my feet and to the East Coast. Recently, we moved to the desert Southwest where we are beginning a new chapter of our lives. I greet each day with a tremendous amount of gratitude for the life with which I've been blessed.

I have a loving, supportive family who overlook my addiction to writing, reading, and the extensions of my hands—my computer to write, or my Kindle Fire to read the stories others write. I'm old enough to know how to have fun but too old to care what others think about my definition of a good time. In my heart and soul, I believe I hit the cosmic jackpot with the life I have, and I thank the Universe for it.

Cheers!

If you enjoyed this book, I'd appreciate it if you'd leave a rating and/or a review at Amazon.com and maybe a kind word on Goodreads. If you have constructive criticism to help me evolve as a writer, please pass it along to me.

You can find me at: https://linktr.ee/SamE.Kraemer
Facebook Profile: Author Sam E. Kraemer
Facebook Reader Group: Kraemer's Klubhouse
Goodreads: Sam on Goodreads

Amazon Author Page: Sam's Amazon Page
BookBub: Sam E. Kraemer, Author
Newsletter: Sam's Newsletter Sign-up
Website: Sam E. Kraemer Website

Whew! I'm everywhere (even on Insta and Twitter. Go to Linktree profile). I'd love to hear from you!

ALSO BY SAM E. KRAEMER

The Lonely Heroes
Ranger Hank
Guardian Gabe

Weighting...
Weighting for Love
Weighting for Laughter
Weighting for a Lifetime

Single Novels
The Secrets We Whisper to the Bees
The Holiday Gamble
Unbreak Him

May-December Hearts Collection
A Wise Heart
Heart of Stone

Elves after Dark & Dawn
My Jingle Bell Heart
Georgie's Eggcellent Adventure

Men of Memphis Blues
Cash & Cary

Made in the USA
Las Vegas, NV
16 June 2022